Battle Royale: Angels' Border

Episodes 1 & 2

Story by Koushun Takami (with N-cake)
Art by Mioko Ohnishi & Youhei Oguma

About the Battle Royale…

This story takes place on an island chain in the Far East under the authority of the Republic of Greater East Asia—a country with its own particular brand of totalitarian rule and a cultural background nearly identical to modern-day Japan. A policy of quasi-seclusion targeting hostile nations, among them America, inhibits travel and the flow of information, and its citizens undergo thorough indoctrination. The Republic restricts literature from enemy states and guards against underground, anti-governmental movements for free and democratic ideals. The slightest suspicion of such revolutionary actions results in harsh punishments, including imprisonment and execution.

Perhaps the best symbol of this country's unique nature is the "Program," a killing game involving junior high students. Said to be a military experiment essential to the nation's defense, the Program's specifics are kept from the general public. All that is known is that an entire ninth grade class is selected each year and the students are forced to kill their classmates. Only the sole survivor is allowed to return home. Each "winner," many of whom subsequently suffer from mental disorders such as PTSD, are forced to relocate and are forbidden from talking about the game.

The test subjects are provided with a bag containing limited rations, a map, and a randomly selected weapon. Each student is fitted with a collar that transmits his or her vitals. Within the designated arena, students have the freedom to move or hide as they please, but explosives in their collars are linked to an ever-expanding list of forbidden zones. Through this forced movement, confrontations become inevitable. And since the collars also broadcast the subjects' whereabouts, escape is impossible. Each experiment runs until only one student remains—unless 24 hours pass without a single death, in which case all the students are killed. Since the students' starting point also serves as the operational headquarters of the supervisors for the experiment, it becomes the first forbidden zone.

BOYS			
1	Yoshio Akamatsu	12	Yutaka Seto
2	Keita Iijima	13	Yuichiro Takiguchi
3	Tatsumichi Oki	14	Sho Tsukioka
4	Toshinori Oda	15	● Shuya Nanahara
5	Shogo Kawada	16	Kazushi Niida
6	Kazuo Kiriyama	17	Mitsuru Numai
7	Yoshitoki Kuninobu	18	Tadakatsu Hatagami
8	Yoji Kuramoto	19	▲ Shinji Mimura
9	Hiroshi Kuronaga	20	Kyoichi Motobuchi
10	Ryuhei Sasagawa	21	Kazuhiko Yamamoto
11	Hiroki Sugimura		

Shiroiwa Town, Kagawa Prefecture

SHIROIWA JUNIOR HIGH

Ninth Grade Class B Roster

EPISODE I: ● EPISODE II: ▲ I & II: ◆

GIRLS			
1	Mizuho Inada	12	● Haruka Tanizawa
2	● Yukie Utsumi	13	Takako Chigusa
3	Megumi Eto	14	Mayumi Tendo
4	Sakura Ogawa	15	Noriko Nakagawa
5	Izumi Kanai	16	● Yuka Nakagawa
6	Yukiko Kitano	17	● Satomi Noda
7	Yumiko Kusaka	18	Fumiyo Fujiyoshi
8	Kayoko Kotohiki	19	◆ Chisato Matsui
9	● Yuko Sakaki	20	Kaori Minami
10	Hirono Shimizu	21	Yoshimi Yahagi
11	Mitsuko Souma		

ONCE THE LAST STUDENT LEAVES THE FACILITY, NONE ARE ALLOWED TO RETURN.

SHUYA NANAHARA, A NINTH GRADER IN CLASS B AT SHIROIWA JUNIOR HIGH, LIVES IN AN ORPHANAGE WITH HIS BEST FRIEND YOSHITOKI KUNINOBU. SHUYA JOINED THE MUSIC CLUB AFTER AN ALTERCATION WITH HIS TEACHER LED TO HIS QUITTING BASEBALL. NOW HE DEVOTES HIMSELF TO ILLEGAL, UNPATRIOTIC MUSIC (ROCK AND ROLL). SHUYA HAS A SENSIBLE NATURE AND IS POPULAR—PARTICULARLY WITH GIRLS. HIS CLASS OF 42 STUDENTS IS EMBARKING ON A SCHOOL TRIP WHEN THEY ARE TAKEN FROM THEIR BUS AND BROUGHT TO OKI ISLAND IN THE SETO INLAND SEA. THE FIRST TO DIE IS SHUYA'S FRIEND, YOSHITOKI KUNINOBU. BUT THE PROGRAM HAS STARTED AND SHUYA HAS NO TIME TO GRIEVE. HE IS ATTACKED BY YOSHIO AKAMATSU, WHO LEFT THE AREA EARLIER. SHUYA ESCAPES WITH THE NEXT STUDENT TO LEAVE, NORIKO NAKAGAWA. LATER, SHOGO KAWADA, THE INTIMIDATING TRANSFER STUDENT WHO WAS HELD BACK A YEAR, SAVES SHUYA'S LIFE AND TELLS THEM THAT HE HAS A WAY TO ESCAPE THE ISLAND. THEY DECIDE TO TRUST HIM, AND THE THREE TEAM UP.

MEANWHILE, BASKETBALL ACE AND HACKER SHINJI MIMURA HAS HIS OWN PLANS TO ESCAPE THE ISLAND. MARTIAL ARTS STUDENT HIROKI SUGIMURA BEGINS WANDERING THE ISLAND IN A PERILOUS SEARCH FOR A CLASSMATE. KAZUO KIRIYAMA, THE MASTERFUL LEADER OF A DELINQUENT GROUP, AND MITSUKO SOUMA, LEADER OF A BAD-GIRL GANG, BEGIN CARRYING OUT THEIR SEPARATE PLANS.

LATE IN THE NIGHT OF MAY 22ND, ROUGHLY 22 HOURS AFTER THE GAME BEGAN, HALF OF THE CLASS IS DEAD. BADLY WOUNDED AND SEPARATED FROM NORIKO AND KAWADA, SHUYA FALLS DOWN A STEEP SLOPE AND LOSES CONSCIOUSNESS IN FRONT OF THE LIGHTHOUSE, WHERE SIX GIRLS, INCLUDING YUKIE UTSUMI, ARE HOLED UP.

ANGELS' BORDER CONTAINS TWO STORIES, NOT PRESENTED IN THE ORIGINAL NOVEL, OF THIS GROUP OF GIRLS.

EPISODE I

ARTIST: MIOKO OHNISHI

EPISODE II

ARTIST: YOUHEI OGUMA

BONUS DOCUMENT

Battle Royale: Angels' Border Original Script

Written by Koushun Takami

Battle Royale: Angels' Border

EPISODE ONE

Art by Mioko Ohnishi

We share our hope.

EPISODE I

Act 1...Think

SHAAAA
SHA-SHAAAA

MAY 23, 3:06 A.M.
SHAAA

SHAAA

TMP
TMP

First...
BOW
BOW
TMP
...there's something you need to know.
TMP
TMP
TMP

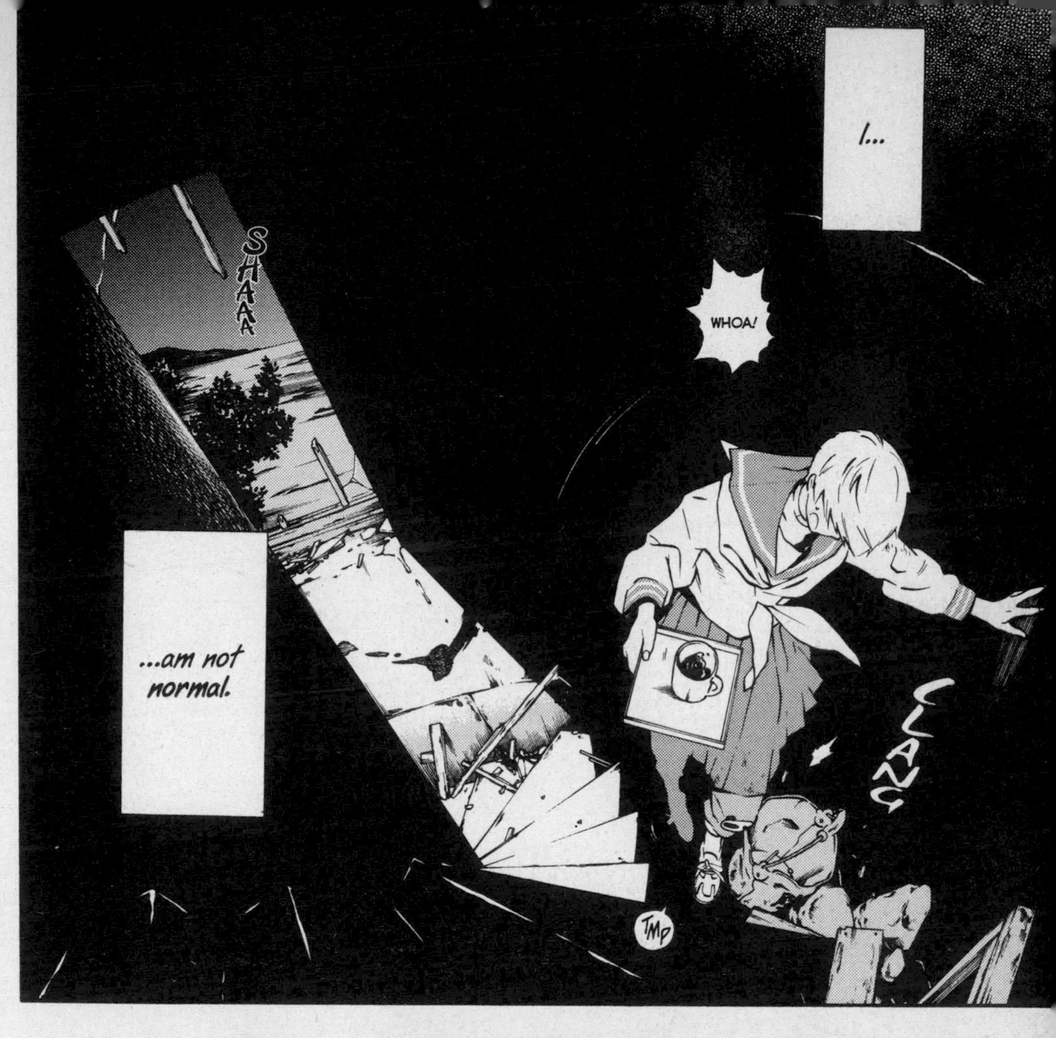
I...
WHOA!
SHAAA
...am not normal.
CLANG
TMP

KEEP IT...
...STEADY.
SPLISH
I haven't come out yet.
UGH, IT'S SO DARK...
?!
FLAP
FLAP FLAP FLAP

FLAP
CAW

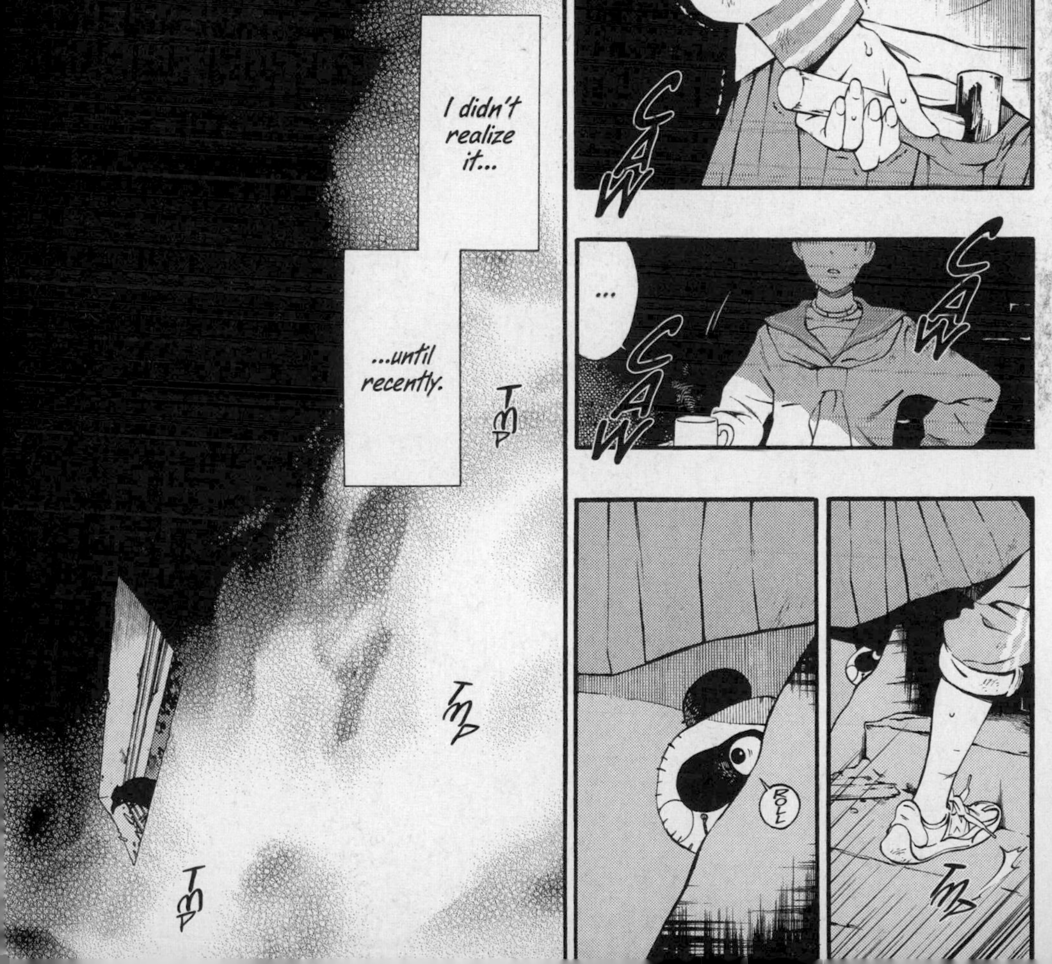
CAW
...
CAW
CAW
ROLL
TMP
I didn't realize it...
...until recently.
TMP
TMP
TMP

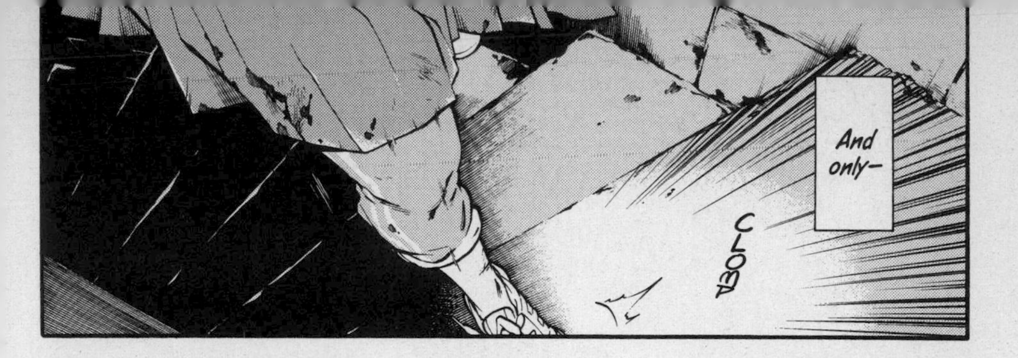
And only—
CLOMP

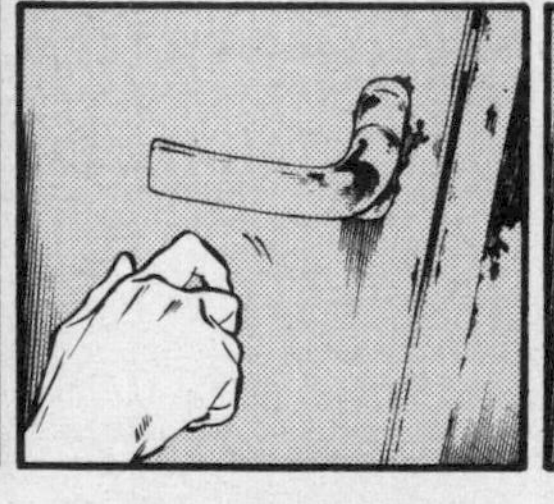

And only...
TMP
TMP

... because of her.
TMP
YUKIE!
CHAK

YUKIE...
HOW ABOUT SOME COFFEE?

SOUNDS GOOD.
YOU MADE MORE?
CLINK

YOU CAN'T DRINK LYING DOWN LIKE THAT.
LET'S TRADE.

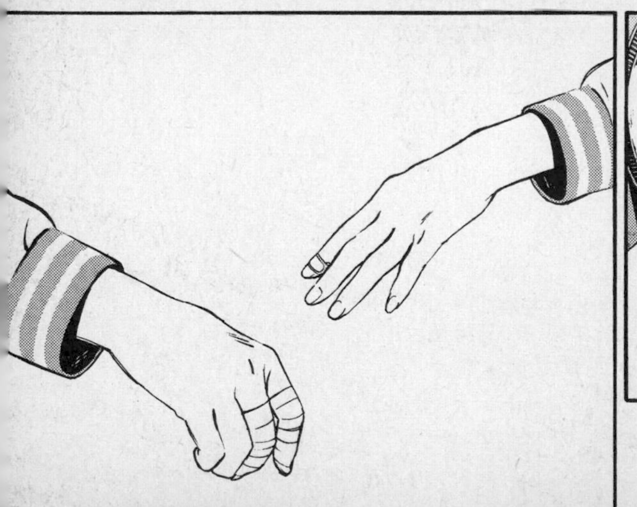

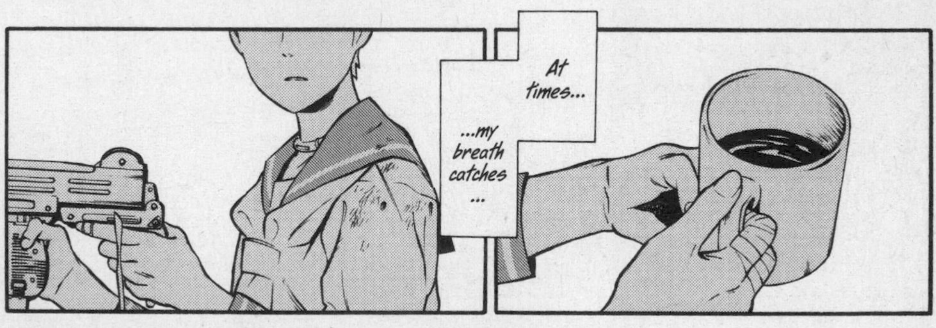
At times...
...my breath catches
...

...in awe that the one I love...
...is so beautiful.

YUKIE!
No, no! This is no time to think like that!
YOUR CHEST– YOU'RE EXPOSING YOURSELF.
WHAT ?

OH... SORRY.
...

WELL ...
AT A TIME LIKE THIS, WE'RE BOUND TO LET OUR-SELVES GO A BIT.

BUT REALLY, YOU NEVER HAVE A HAIR OUT OF PLACE.
YOU'RE OUR CLASS LEADER, AFTER ALL.
AND ...

...YOUR FATHER IS SO STRICT.

OH ...
OH, NO!

...
The one I love...
...doesn't like it when people mention her father.

He's a soldier in the Non-Aggressive Forces.
Hardly anyone knows. Not in class or even on our volley-ball team.

Soldiers aren't much loved in this country, partly because of a certain military research program.

And right now...
...we're in it.
I'm taking this watch very seriously.

Watch-ing...
...in case anyone comes to kill us.

And if anyone comes to kill us...

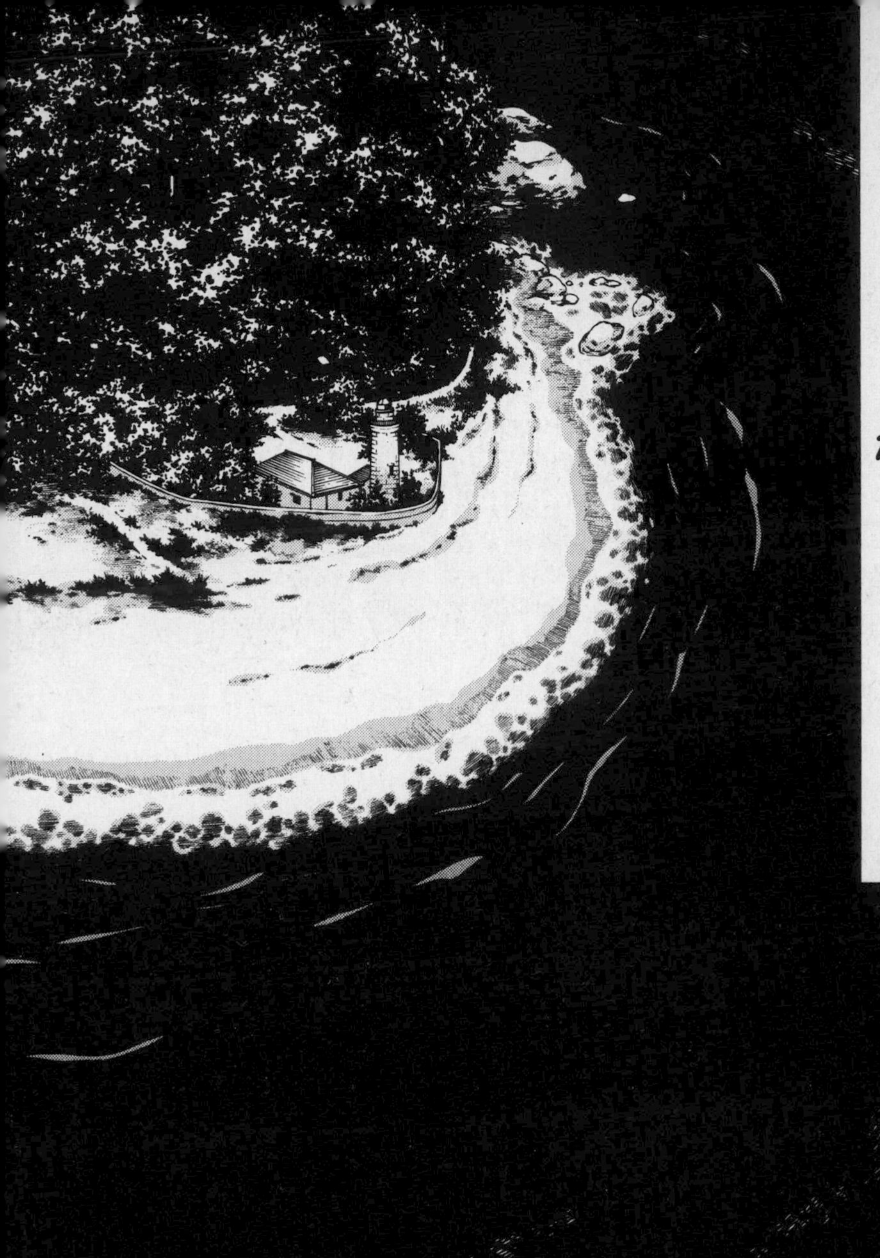

...I have to kill them.

The forty-two of us in Shiroiwa Junior High Ninth Grade Class B thought we were going on a school trip. Instead, we were drugged.
It was around one in the morning when we awoke inside a school on an island we'd never seen before...
KINPAT
SKR
SKR
Over twenty-four hours have passed since then.
ALL RIGHT, EVERYONE, DID YOU SLEEP WELL?
In that classroom, a strange man named Sakamochi told us we were about to begin the Program.
NOW NOW, EVERYONE SETTLE DOWN.
CLACK
?!
I'LL EXPLAIN EVERY-THING.

TODAY...
...YOU'RE ALL GOING TO KILL EACH OTHER!
ISN'T THAT GREAT! ♡

THE LAST ONE ALIVE GETS TO GO HOME.
The Program ...
MURMUR
MURMUR
That's what they call the annual military test conducted in the Republic of Greater East Asia, our country.

One ninth-grade class is chosen at random.

The students kill each other for the sole survivor's seat.

I still don't understand what they're testing, but I've known about it for as long as I can remember.

THIS YEAR, THIRTY-EIGHT STUDENTS HAVE DIED.
A GIRL HAS BEEN ANNOUNCED THE WINNER...
But ...

...I never imagined ...
...that my class would be chosen.
It's probably that way for everybody.
Like a car accident ...
...or a bad illness.
"This can't be happen-ing!"

But this was no prank.
AHHH !!
Pranks don't end with someone dying.
THUD
NOO !!

Our homeroom teacher, Mr. Hayashida, tried to protect us.
And two of us, Yoshitoki Kuninobu and Fumiyo Fujiyoshi ...
...were killed on the spot for disobeying orders.

SHAAAA

...

SO ...
THIS IS A MACHINE GUN, HUH? HEAVY, ISN'T IT?
YEAH.
YOU KNOW ...

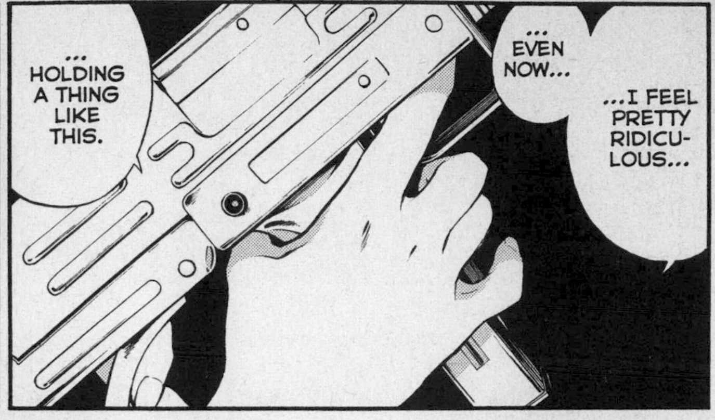
...EVEN NOW...
...I FEEL PRETTY RIDICULOUS...
...HOLDING A THING LIKE THIS.

YEAH, BUT...
CLACK

...IF I HADN'T HAD MINE, WE MIGHT NOT HAVE MET UP.

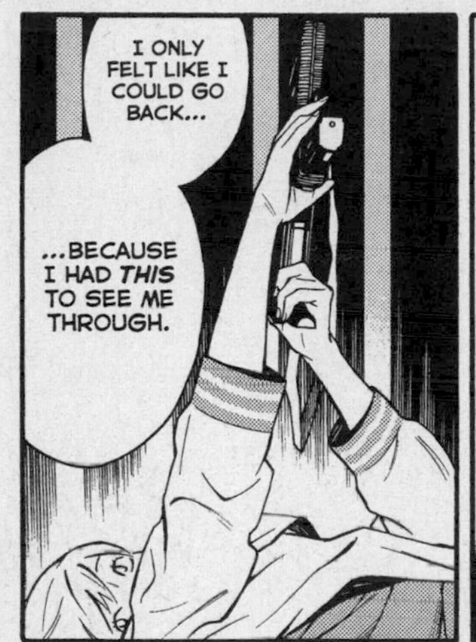
I ONLY FELT LIKE I COULD GO BACK...
...BECAUSE I HAD *THIS* TO SEE ME THROUGH.

When the test began, we left by seat order, one by one. Everyone else on the island had been evacuated by the government.
Disoriented, I ran through the still night.
HUFF
HUFF
HUFF

But then I heard someone call my name.
HARUKA.
HARUKA...
EEK!
JOLT

HARUKA.
OVER HERE!
Again, it's the rules that every classmate is your enemy.
HARUKA!

But Yukie and I have been playing volleyball together ever since elementary school.

She as setter, and me as hitter.

TRIP
YUKI–
HARUKA, WATCH OUT!

THUD

C'MON, HARUKA! YOU'RE TOO HEAVY.
YOU KNOW YOU'RE BIGGER THAN ME!
CLENCH

YUKIE ... I'M SO GLAD ...
I'M SO GLAD.

SO GLAD ...
Anyway, I can trust her.
... YEAH.
Yukie would *never* try to kill me.
YEAH ...

And Yukie trusts me, too.
And that makes me feel so...
...
TMP
TMP

... HEY, HARUKA?
WHAT ?

GASP
OH! SORRY, YUKIE!
SCRAMBLE

Before we left the school, we each got a weapon and some food.
My weapon was a hammer.
But Yukie had a pistol.
...

YUKIE ?
SHUP

KA CHAK

YUKI–

LET'S GO BACK, HARUKA!

HUH?
LET'S GO BACK TO THE SCHOOL.
WITH THIS GUN, WE'LL BE SAFE.
HERE, READ THIS.
OH.

E-EVERYONE? EVERYONE?!
WE ALL NEED TO COME UP WITH A PLAN.

THAT WAS SCARY.
AND THEN WE CAN CALL OUT TO EVERYONE.

...
COME ON, GET UP.
LET'S GO, HARUKA.
TAP

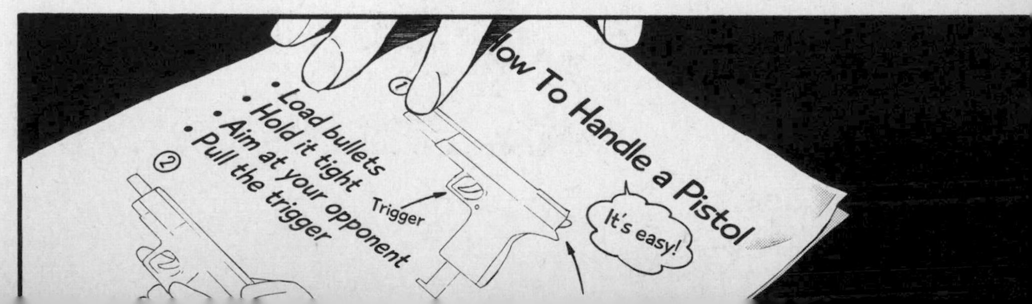
How To Handle a Pistol
①
• Load bullets
• Hold it tight
• Aim at your opponent
• Pull the trigger
Trigger
It's easy!
②

OF COURSE I'M SCARED.

I MEAN...
...YOU HEARD WHAT THAT MAN SAID IN THE CLASS-ROOM.

THE OTHERS ARE READY TO KILL.

ARE YOU LISTENING, CLASS?
!

EVERY-ONE'S FACES...
IT WAS SO SCARY.
AND YET...

IT'S STILL HARD TO BELIEVE ANY OF US WOULD TRY TO KILL EACH OTHER.

CONSIDERING WHAT HAPPENED TO YUMIKO AND YUKIKO...
That was yesterday morning.
From a mountaintop observation deck, the two girls called out to stop all this.
EVERY-ONE! STOP FIGHT-ING!
COME UP HERE!
CHISATO! WHERE'S THAT VOICE COMING FROM?
UP IN THE MOUN-TAINS!
NONE OF US WANT TO FIGHT.

IT'S YUMIKO AND YUKI-

WHAT?

YUMIKO!
BRATATATATAT
YUKIKO!
AIEEEE!

...YOU MEAN THE GOVERNMENT DID IT?
LIKE WITH HIDDEN SOLDIERS?
YEAH...

BUT THERE'S AKAMATSU AND NIIDA, TOO.
When we returned to the school, we saw two dead bodies.

From a distance, we couldn't see much, but when Yuka Nakagawa joined us, she said...
...arrows were sticking out of their bodies.

And we'd just seen Kazushi Niida running away holding something that could've been a bow...
AKAMATSU WAS THE FIRST TO LEAVE, BUT HE CAME BACK...

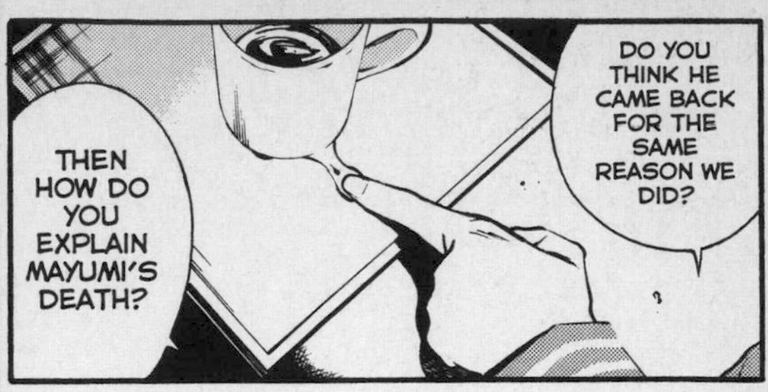
DO YOU THINK HE CAME BACK FOR THE SAME REASON WE DID?
THEN HOW DO YOU EXPLAIN MAYUMI'S DEATH?

COULDN'T AKAMATSU HAVE SUDDENLY RUN INTO TENDO?
YOU KNOW HOW EASILY SPOOKED AKAMATSU IS...
...MAYBE HE JUST PANICKED AND PULLED THE TRIGGER.

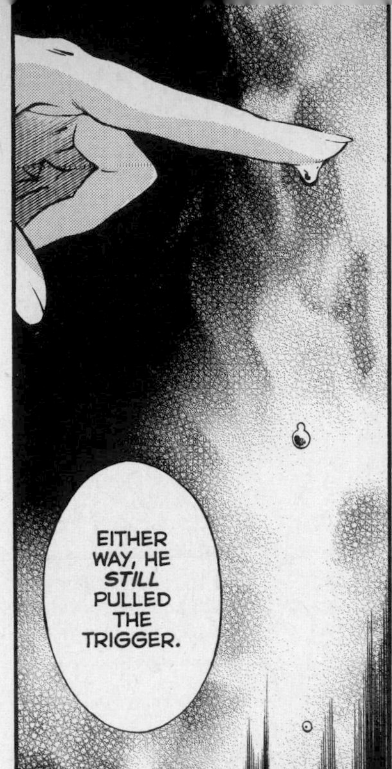
EITHER WAY, HE *STILL* PULLED THE TRIGGER.

WHATEVER THE REASON, NIIDA MUST'VE KILLED AKAMATSU.
AND ...

...
...

"AND ...
SKRITCH
"...THERE'S WHAT YUKO SAID ABOUT NANAHARA," RIGHT?
Due in part to what we'd seen, we decided to only call out to the girls.

Skipping the boys, we had...
... Yuka ...
... Satomi Noda...
... Chisato Matsui ...
YUKIE!
GIRLS!

Kaori Minami was next, but she ran when she saw us.
I can't blame her.
In this game, being in a group isn't proof of good intentions.

Anyone could turn on you at any moment.
Or you could turn on each other...
Yoshimi Yahagi was the last one out, but we didn't call out to her.

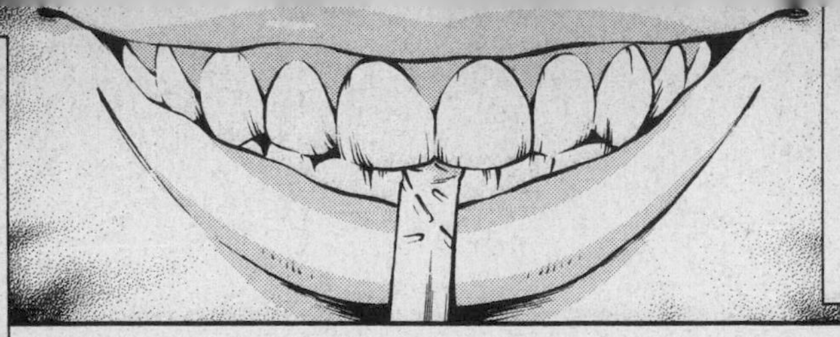
She's one of Mitsuko Souma's bad girls.
That was the only reason.

FROM THE HIGHLANDS
STRAWBERRY
MILK

THIS PLACE IS CONSPIC-UOUS...
I KEEP THINKING SOMEONE WILL COME AGAIN.
AT LEAST WE CAN SEE THEM IF THEY DO.

YEAH, I GUESS...

IT'S LIKE WE'RE...
SHAAAA
...A NATION.

A NATION?
YEAH.
WE'VE SHUT OURSELVES IN HERE, CHOOSING WHO WE LET IN AND WHO WE EXCLUDE.
...

EVEN BEFORE WE CAME HERE, WE'D ALREADY EXCLUDED YAHAGI.

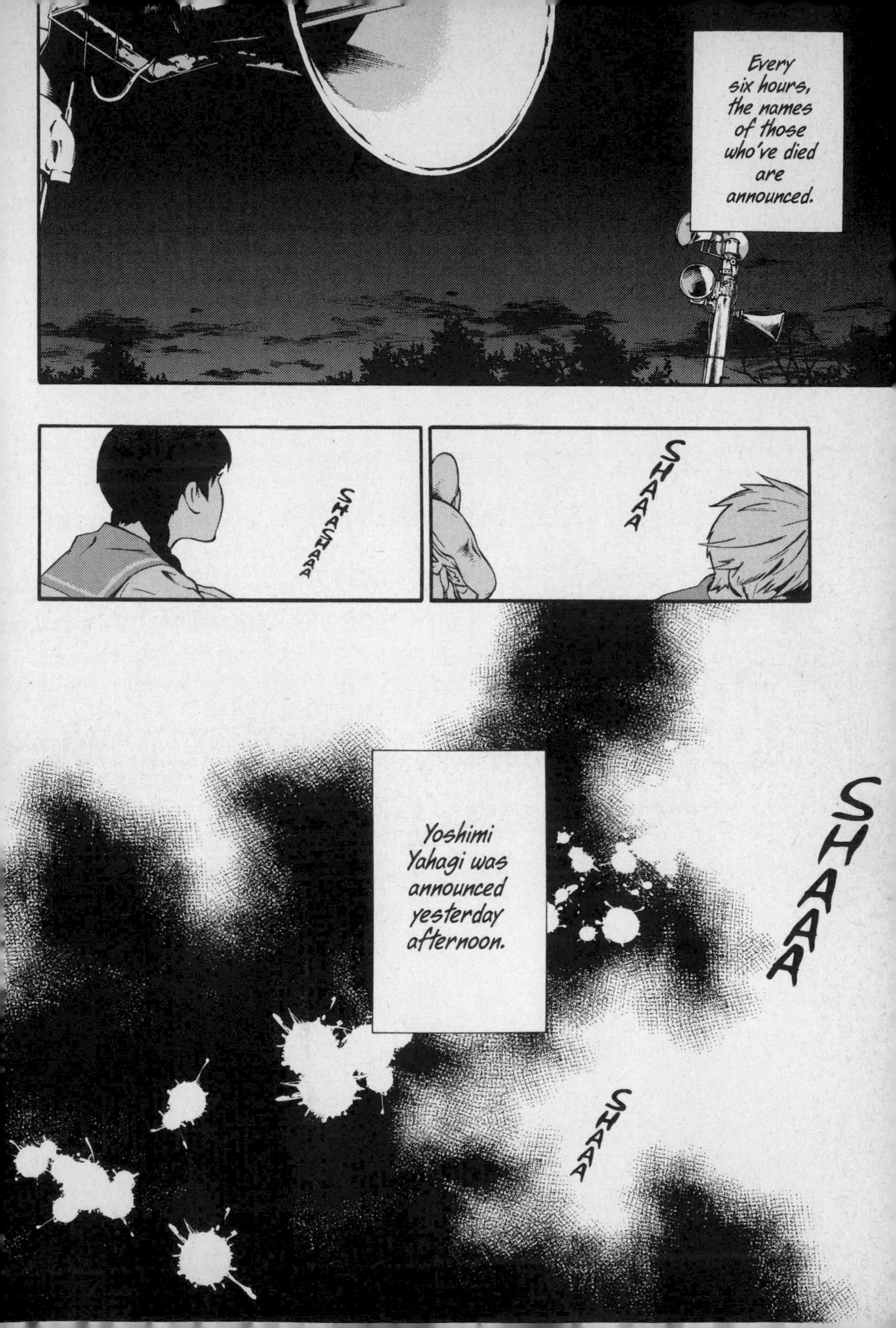
Every six hours, the names of those who've died are announced.
SHAAA
SHASHAAA
SHAAA
Yoshimi Yahagi was announced yesterday afternoon.
SHAAA

SHASHAAA
MAY 23, 11:32 A.M.
SHAAA
URGH...
SKSSH SKSSH

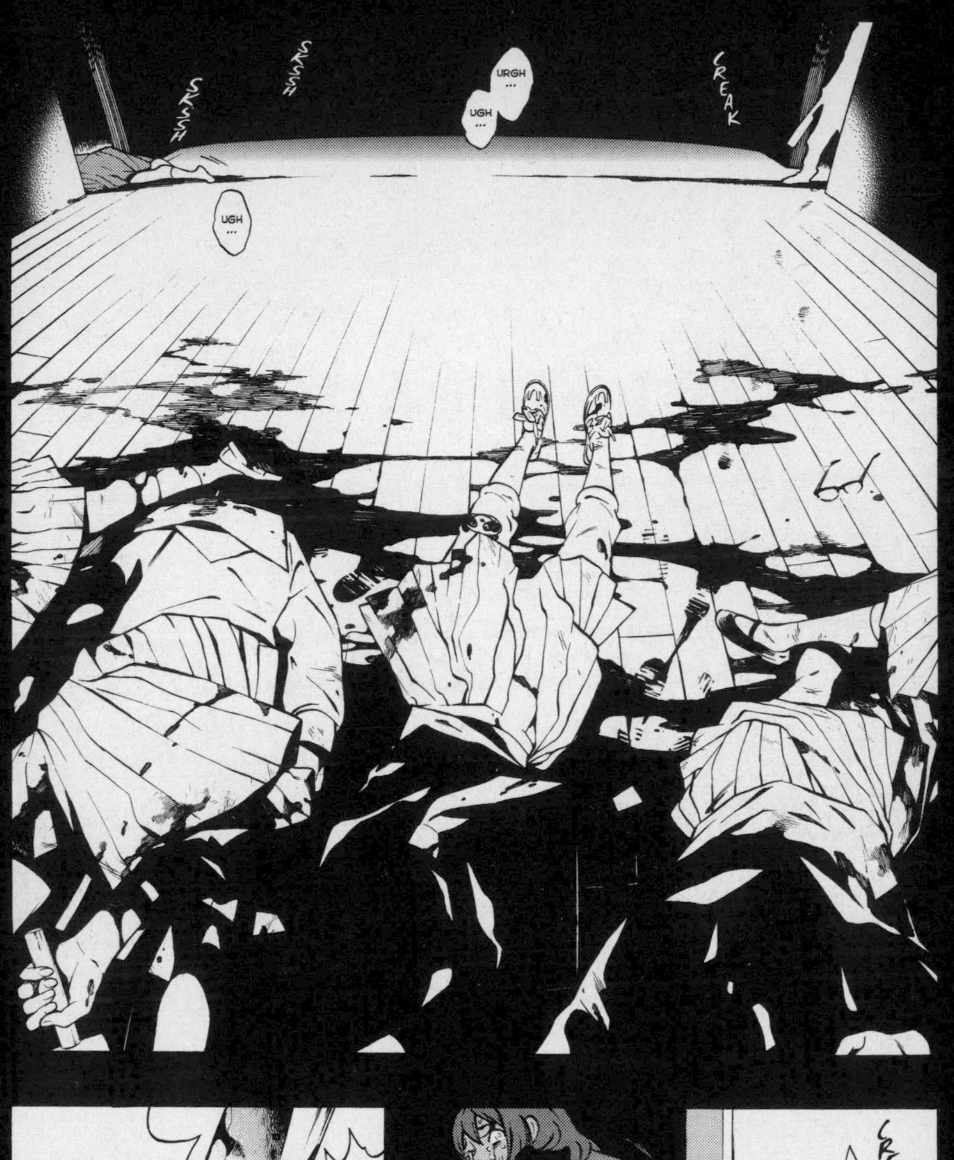
CREAK
URGH...
UGH...
SKSSH
SKSSH
UGH...

CREAK
HEL...
CREAK
SOME-ONE...
HELP...
ME...
PLIP
EEEII-IAAAH-HH!!

YUKO?
GAWA
YOU WERE SPACING OUT THERE. ARE YOU OKAY?
UH ...
YEAH ...
I'M GOING TO MAKE SOME STEW.
PERFECT! GET SOME-THING WARM IN YOUR STOMACH— THAT'LL CALM YOUR NERVES.
YUKA, THAT'S JUST YOU.
YAWN...
...
WHAT'S THAT SUPPOSED TO MEAN?
HA HA HA HA HA
THUMP
THUMP THUMP
HUFF
THUMP
HUFF

HUFF
HUFF
HUFF
HUFF
HUFF
CAUTION
THIS IS POISON. DEATH IS IMMEDIATE.
FATAL DOSAGE: 0.15G
SHAAA

EPISODE I

Act 2...Hurt

SHAAA

May 23, 3:15 A.M.

...

NOD

After the five of us left the school, we wandered the island.

When we came near the island's northern edge...
WAIT, WHERE'S YUKIE?
SHE'S TAKING A LOOK BEYOND THE TREELINE AHEAD.
SHE'S ALONE? BUT THAT'S DANGEROUS!
YUKIE!
YUKIE?

THAT'S WEIRD... WHY IS THERE CLOVER SCATTERED AROUND?
HARUKA... I...I SAW...
YUKIE?
YUKIE?!
She saw...

...Kazuhiko Yamamoto and Sakura Ogawa, who had been the closest couple in class...
...tossing themselves off the cliff into the sea.

They must've found a way to meet here...
...so they could leave the game together.

HMM ...
...
I wonder if they were happy to die with the one they loved.

I wonder if Yukie is thinking of the boy she's in love with.

Eventually we arrived at this lighthouse.
Once we were sure that no one was inside, we decided to hole up here.

We barricaded the door...
...and assigned the guard rotation first thing.
We had no electricity or gas, but the water tank held a reserve.
We found some fuel tablets to cook with.

The afternoon was my turn to sleep.
Then night came again.
HEY, LOOK, HARUKA.
I FOUND A BATTERY-OPERATED PORTABLE RADIO. AND SOME EMERGENCY FOOD IN POUCHES.
THIS PLACE IS PRETTY WELL-STOCKED.

Of course, the body count continued to rise.
BEEP
RATTLE RATTLE
?!

AHEM ...

IT'S TIME FOR ANNOUNCEMENTS.
THESE ARE YOUR FRIENDS WHO ARE NOW DEAD!
NIIDA, CHIGUSA, AND MINAMI.

OH, I FORGOT. TSUKIOKA TOO.
RATTLE RATTLE BEEP

TAKAKO ...
KAORI... TSUKIOKA ...
Not long after that, two of our other classmates wound up here.
CREAM STEW

They came, of course, by chance.
HEY, LOOK!
IS THAT YUKO?

YUKO!
?!
JOLT
YUKO!
YUKO!
EEP!

AH ...
TREMBLE
TREMBLE
AH ...
AH ...
TREMBLE

EEEEE-IIIIII-AAAAA!!
YUKO!
IT'S ALL RIGHT. LOOK.
EEEIII-AAA!
EEEIII-AAA!
QUIET! BE QUIET. OKAY?
First was Yuko Sakaki, at around eight last night.

She was half-delirious—we practically took her in under protective custody.

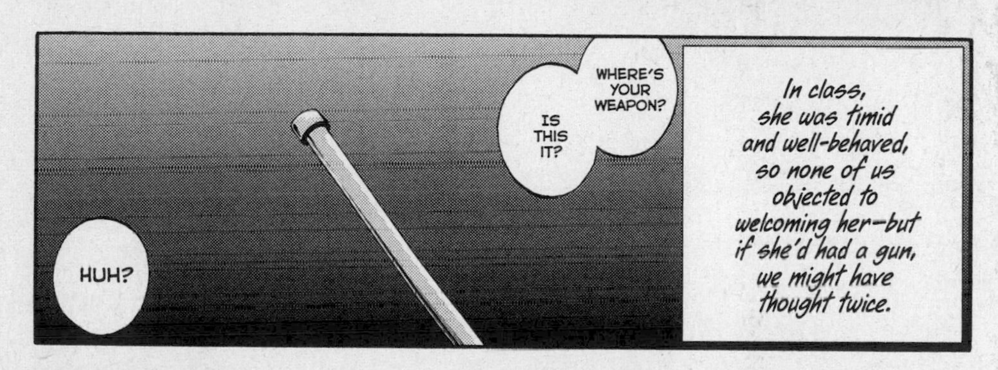
In class, she was timid and well-behaved, so none of us objected to welcoming her—but if she'd had a gun, we might have thought twice.
WHERE'S YOUR WEAPON?
IS THIS IT?
HUH?

YEAH, IT IS. JUST... THIS.
YEAH.
OKAY.
CLUTCH

HARUKA HAD A HAMMER, OF ALL THINGS.
IT'S TRUE! WHAT WAS I SUPPOSED TO DO WITH THAT?
BUT LOOK HERE.

IT CAME IN HANDY WITH THE BARRI-CADES.
HA HA HA HA
YOU SAID IT.
...
Then, four hours later...

...while I was keeping watch...
!
BRATTATATATATA

GUN-FIRE?
SAME AS BEFORE ...

IT'S HAPPENING AGAIN ...
SOME-WHERE... SOMEONE IS...
CRASH SNAP CRASH

RUSTLE
THUD
WHAT ?

PEEK
WH-WHAT ...

SOME-ONE'S ON THE GROUND ...
DID HE FALL DOWN THE SLOPE?
IS THAT...

OH!

He was badly injured, but deciding whether or not to let him in caused a bit of turmoil. Actually getting outside was a problem too, but more than that...

WHOEVER DID THAT TO HIM MIGHT BE NEARBY.
THUD
BUT...

HE'S NOT MOVING! I'M GOING TO TAKE A LOOK.
WHAT ARE YOU TALKING ABOUT?

WE'LL WAIT TWO MINUTES.
CREAK
THEN HARUKA AND I WILL GO *TOGETHER*.
!

ALL RIGHT.
SOME-BODY GO UP TOP AND GIVE US COVER, SO–
NO !!
?!

HE'LL KILL YOU!
HE'LL KILL US ALL!

Yuko told us she saw Nanahara kill Tatsumichi Oki.
He split open Oki's head with a hatchet.
...

Even if she did see what she thought she saw... knowing Nanahara...
We all naturally assumed it must have been an accident.
But Yuko wouldn't listen.

In the end...
...we agreed to keep him locked in a room, and then we brought him inside.

But we couldn't tell if he'd even wake up again.

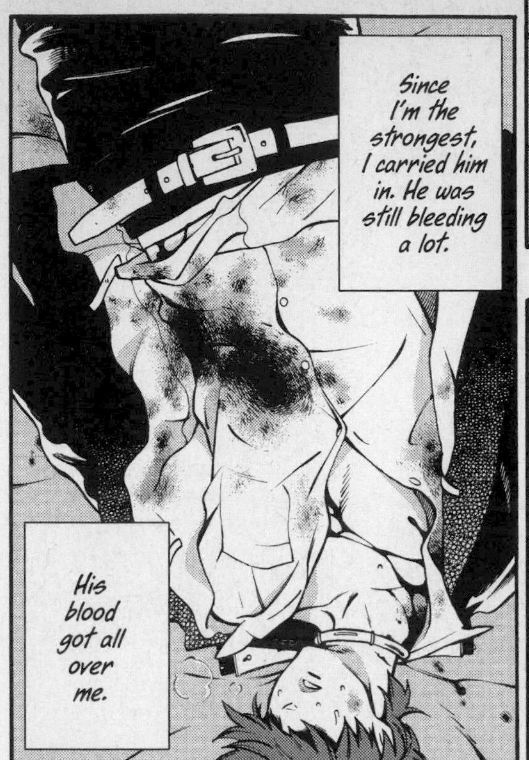
Since I'm the strongest, I carried him in. He was still bleeding a lot.
His blood got all over me.

SNIFF, SNIFF

I WANT TO WASH MY CLOTHES.
I WANT TO TAKE A BATH.
SIGH
...

Anyway, we brought Nanahara inside...
...and saw to his wounds.

HARUKA!
COVER THE WINDOWS SO THE LIGHT WON'T SPILL OUT.
RIGHT!

CHISATO! BRING ME A NEEDLE AND THREAD.
I HAVE A SEWING KIT IN MY BAG.
ON IT!

YUKA! DO WE STILL HAVE HOT WATER?
OKAY!
IF YOU HAVE TO BOIL MORE, MAKE SURE TO HIDE THE LIGHT!
...
HANG IN THERE, NANA-HARA!

YOU'RE GOING TO BE ALL RIGHT!
Nanahara is cheerful and kind.
He's athletic, and good at playing the guitar.

And he's good-looking too.
PASS ME THE BALL, YOSHITOKI!
NANAHARA

So of course he was popular with the girls.
YAAY!
NANAHARA IS SO COOL!
DON'T YOU THINK, HARUKA?
SURE ...
YEAH, HE IS...
Like I said before, I'm not normal, so none of that matters to me...

But now, in this particular case, I needed to respect Yukie's feelings...
WHAM
WHAM
WHAM
NANA-HARA.
NANA-HARA.

NANA-HARA ...
TANIZAWA

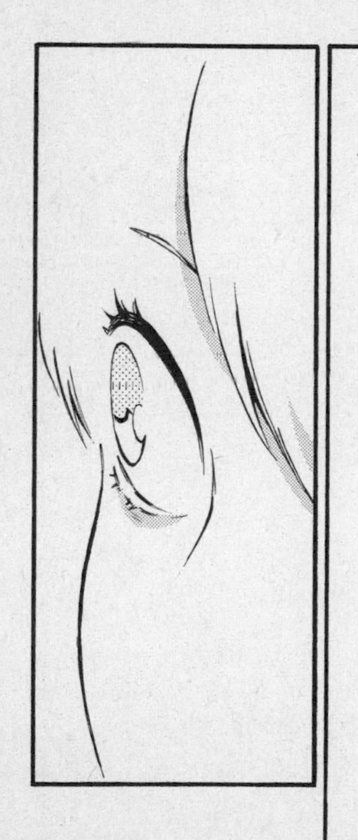

Because I knew she was in love with him.
WHAM
YOW!
THAT HURTS.
SORRY, YUKIE, I'M GOING TO NEED...
YUKIE?
And...

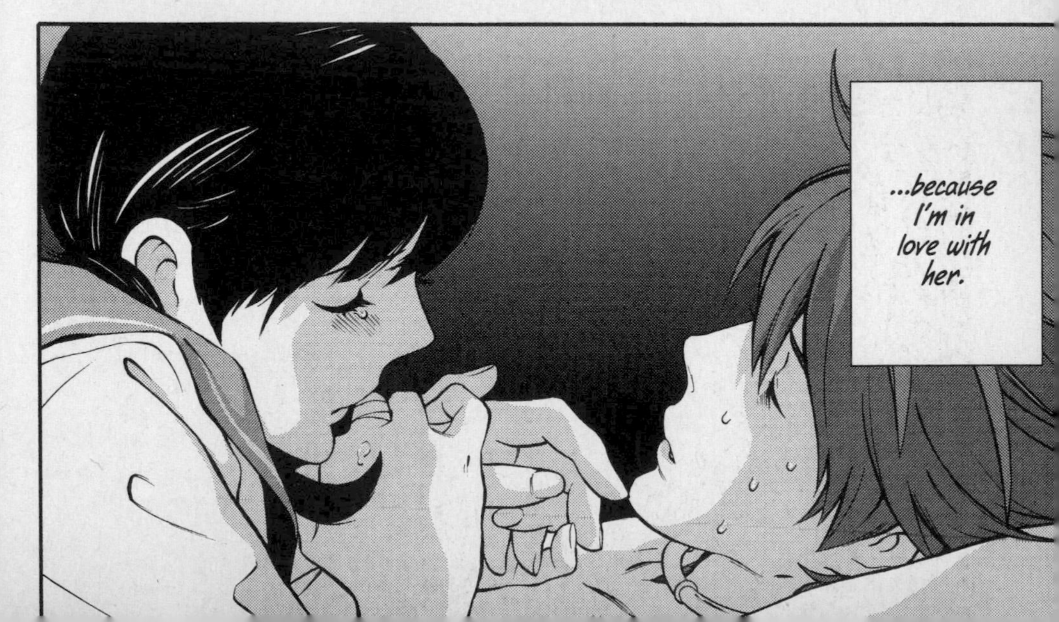
...because I'm in love with her.

Deeply.

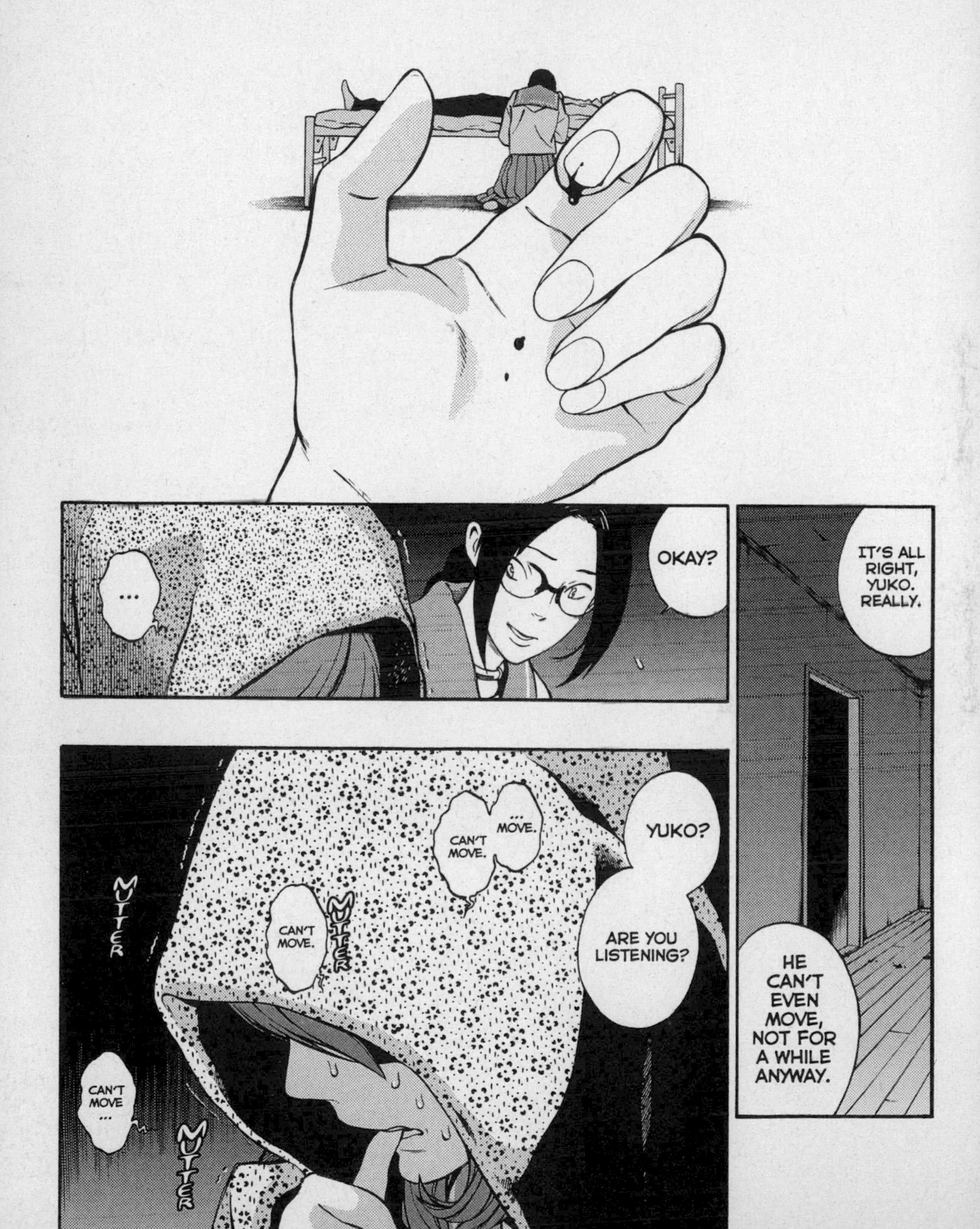

IT'S ALL RIGHT, YUKO. REALLY.
OKAY?
...
HE CAN'T EVEN MOVE, NOT FOR A WHILE ANYWAY.
YUKO?
ARE YOU LISTENING?
... MOVE.
CAN'T MOVE.
CAN'T MOVE.
MUTTER
MUTTER
CAN'T MOVE ...
MUTTER

MAY 23, 1:08 P.M.

AW, WHAT'D YOU DO THAT FOR, YUKA?
YOU'RE SO CLUMSY.
ALL RIGHT, CLEAN IT UP AND WE'LL ...
SPLATTER
SPLATTER
SPLATTER
YU-
YUKA?

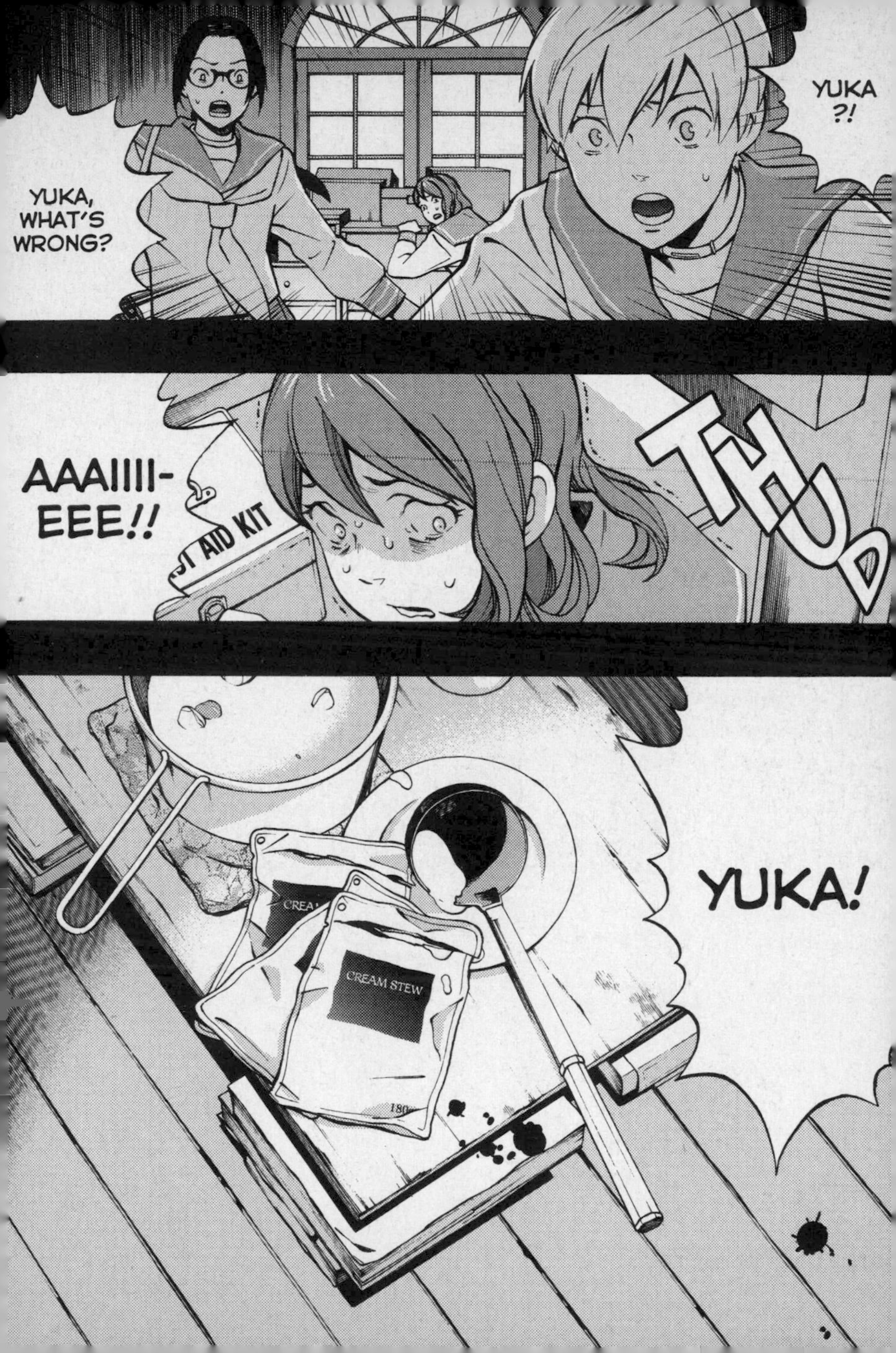
YUKA ?!
YUKA, WHAT'S WRONG?
THUD
AAAIIII-EEE!!
AID KIT
YUKA!
CREAM STEW
180

MAY 23, 3:20 A.M.

EPISODE I

Act 3...Yearn

GO DOWN-STAIRS AND REST.
YOU LOOK SO TIRED.
BUT...
I TOLD YOU I CAN HANDLE THIS. WHERE'S THE TRUST, HUH?
I'M NOT GOING TO SLEEP.
THIS IS A SCHOOL TRIP, AFTER ALL...
HUH?
YOU SEE, I...

...I HAD THIS THOUGHT...I WAS WORRIED THAT...
...MAYBE YOU'RE SICK OF ME.

WHAT?! WHY?
THAT'S NOT TRUE AT ALL!
YEAH, I KNOW.

BUT, IT'S JUST LIKE...
...YOU'VE BEEN DISTANT, MAYBE.
IT'S FELT THAT WAY FOR A WHILE NOW.
...
Truthfully, I sort of knew what she meant...

During a volleyball match, teammates share a physical camaraderie.

For example girls often hug or high five each other after scoring a point.

BOUNCE
But after I realized what I felt toward Yukie...
...it became awkward.
SHIROIWA WINS!

WE DID IT! WE'RE GOING TO THE FINALS!
YAY!
To be blunt...

...I was very aware that I wanted to feel the touch of her body.

Not as a teammate.
I just wanted to feel her touch.
Roman-tically.
HARUKA!
WE DID IT!

...

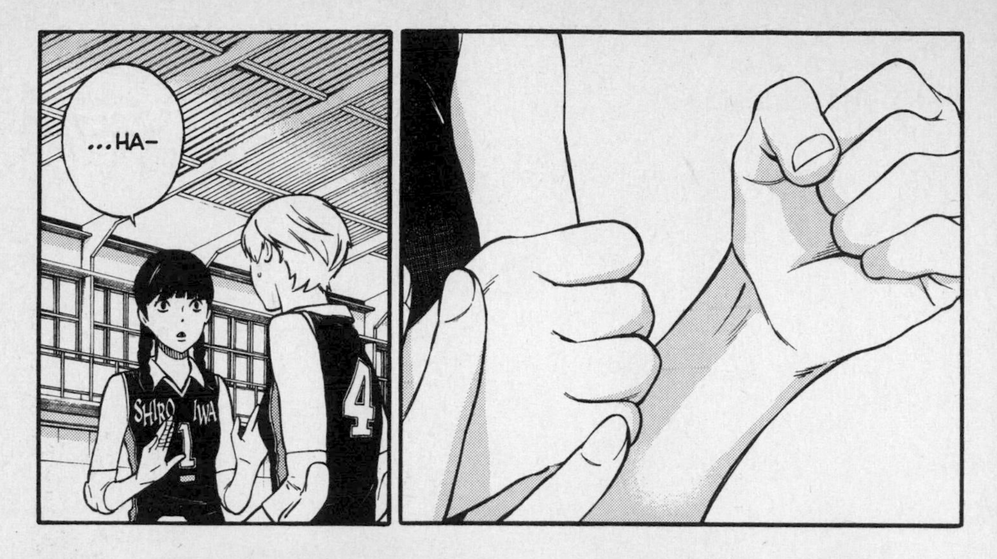
...HA-

HARUKA ...?
HEY, EVERY-ONE!
GATHER UP.
And so...

AH, COM-ING!
LET'S GO, YUKIE.
OH... OKAY.
And so... I felt like I couldn't let her touch me.
TMP

She was pure.
And I didn't want her to get dirty by touching someone like me.

Yesterday, I lost myself and fell into her arms, but...
N-
NO, THAT'S NOT IT.
LOOK, DIDN'T YOU TELL ME?

YOU KNOW...
...THAT CREEP WHO FELT YOU UP.
HOW HE ACTED INNOCENT, THEN THREATENED YOU.
YOU SAID IT MADE YOU FEEL AWFUL.
...YEAH.
WHAT ABOUT IT?
She told me the story around the same time I noticed my feelings for her.
CLACK
CLACK

STOP IT!

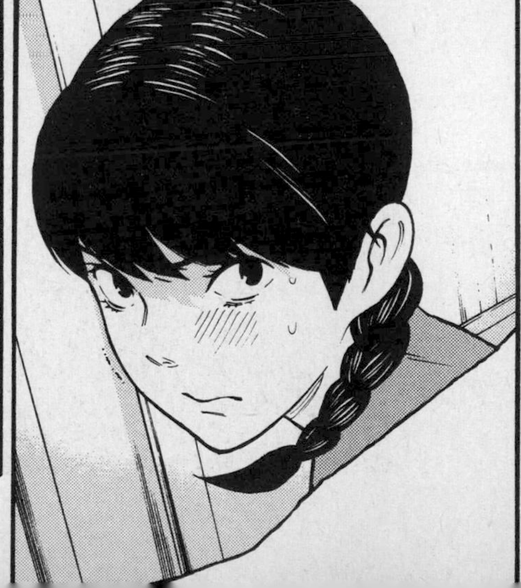

WH-
CHAT-TER

WHAT?
SHE'S LYING!
GIVE ME A BREAK HERE.

YOU ALL SAW!
I HAD BOTH HANDS ON MY NEWSPAPER THE WHOLE TIME!
RIGHT?

!
HMPH.
KIDS THESE DAYS THINK EVERY-THING'S ABOUT THEM.

...
THAT MAN...
ROOM A

WHEN HE WAS GETTING OFF THE TRAIN, HE WHISPERED TO ME.

SPEAK OUT LIKE THAT NEXT TIME...
...AND I'LL KILL YOU, YOU LITTLE SHIT.

TMP

SLAM
SLIDE
SLIIIIIDE

IT'S AWFUL.
I FEEL SO AWFUL, HARUKA.

YUKIE...

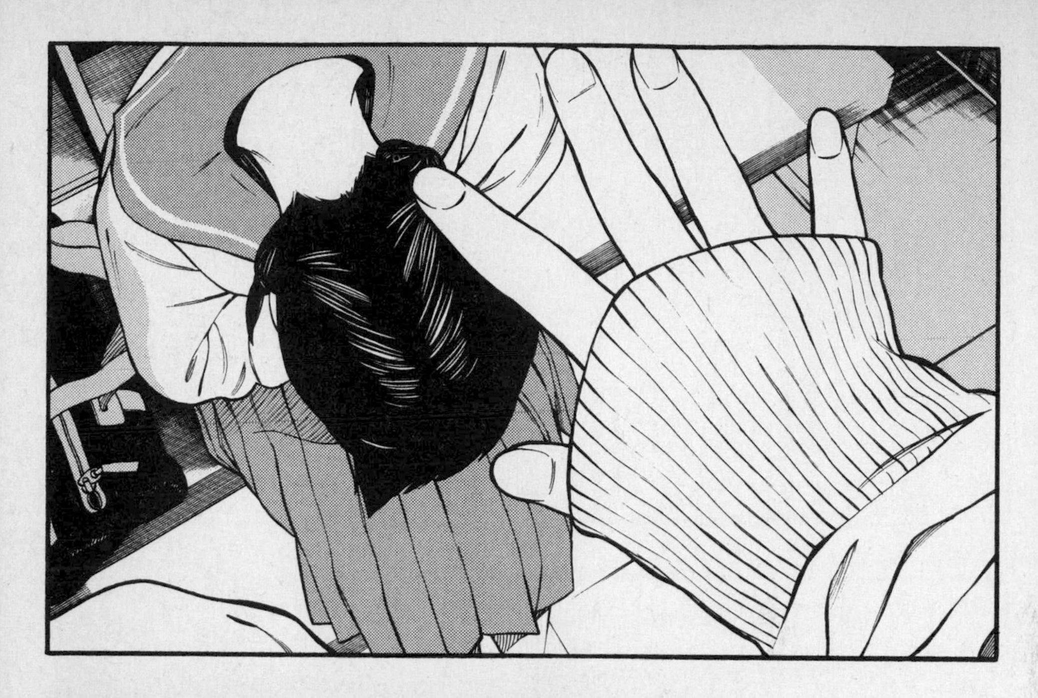

Seeing her that way made me all the more aware of my feelings.
A-AND SO, AFTER THAT, I THOUGHT...
...YOU MIGHT NOT WANT ANYONE TO TOUCH YOU.
WHAT?

YOU'RE TOTALLY DIFFER-ENT!
HE'S SOME CREEPY MAN I DON'T KNOW, AND YOU'RE A GIRL WHO'S MY FRIEND!
TH- THERE'S CREEPY GIRLS TOO, YOU KNOW!
LIKE RIGHT HERE ...
WELL ...

NO, THAT'S DIFFER-ENT TOO.
'CAUSE MEN ARE STRONGER, RIGHT?
NOTHING'S LOWER THAN SOMEONE WHO DOES SOMETHING NASTY JUST BECAUSE THEIR VICTIM CAN'T STOP THEM.

BUT THERE ARE STRONG WOMEN TOO, RIGHT?
LIKE ME...

M-MY GRIP STRENGTH IS 84 POUNDS.
THAT'S MY RIGHT. MY LEFT IS-
C'MON, HARUKA.

WE'RE NOT *THAT* DIFFERENT. MAYBE YOU'RE TALLER THAN ME, BUT...
...YOU'RE MORE FEMININE AND DELICATE.
!
YOU'RE A VERY PRETTY GIRL.
YOU NEED TO HAVE CONFIDENCE.

B... BUT...
WELL, NOW I GET IT.

FROM NOW ON, YOU CAN TOUCH ME ALL THE TIME.
T- TOUCH YOU...
BLUSH

WELL ...
WHO KNOWS HOW MUCH LONGER WE'LL HAVE, ANYWAY.

This game has a time limit.

It goes on until only one of us is left alive.
But if twenty-four hours pass without a single death...
...these collars clamped around our necks explode.

There's more—this island is partitioned into a grid. Each announcement includes an ever-expanding list of sectors we have to avoid... Being in an off-limits sector will also trigger the explosives.
As time passes, less and less of the island will be open to us.
We don't know when this lighthouse will be designated forbidden.
Even if it's still accessible by the time everyone else is dead and only the seven of us here remain...

...unless we kill each other, we'll only have twenty-four hours.

In other words, we have no hope.
We can die together ...
...or we can draw a lottery, and six of us will kill ourselves so that one can live.
IF THAT HAPPENS ...
I'D WANT YUKIE TO SURVIVE.
BUT I KNOW ...
...Yukie wouldn't be able to bear Nanahara's death.

Just as I wouldn't be able to bear hers.
ANYWAY, I DIDN'T KNOW YOU WERE BEING SO CONSIDERATE OF ME.

I WAS STARTING TO THINK I WAS THE ONE ACTING FUNNY—ALWAYS BEING SO CLINGY.
I FELT A LITTLE LONELY.
BUT ...

...WHEN I FIRST SAW YOU YESTERDAY, I WAS SO RELIEVED.
I KNEW I COULD COUNT ON YOU.

IF NOT FOR YOU, I DON'T THINK I WOULD'VE BEEN ABLE...
...TO SEEK OUT THE OTHERS.

YOU'RE MY *BEST FRIEND*, HARUKA.
ISN'T IT JUST LIKE A SCHOOL TRIP TO MAKE YOU FIGURE THAT OUT?

...
YOU REALLY ARE INCREDIBLE, YUKIE.
ME?

YOU'VE GOT SUCH COMPOSURE. OUT HERE, MOST PEOPLE COULDN'T THINK LIKE THAT.
REALLY? I WONDER.

REALLY.
Of course ...

That part of her...
...is just one of the reasons I love Yukie.

YOU'RE MY BEST FRIEND.

YOU'RE MY FRIEND.
STING...

WHO DID IT?
WHO POISONED THE STEW?
MAY 23, 1:10 P.M.
WHICH ONE OF YOU TRIED TO KILL US?

AH...
I...
I...
CREAM STE
WAS IT YOU, CHISATO?
N-
CHAK
NO! I JUST TASTED IT MYSELF!
BUT NOTHING HAPPENED TO ME.
THIS DOESN'T MAKE ANY SENSE...
PUT THE GUN DOWN, SATOMI.
THIS IS ALL A MISUNDER-STANDING.
RATTLE
!

MISUNDER-
STANDING?
HUFF
HUFF
...

Episode I

Act 4...Hope

May 23, 3:26 A.M.

...

...KA.

HARUKA.

HUH? WHAT?
I SAID ...

I WONDER WHAT EVERYONE'S UP TO BELOW.

OH, UMM...
CHISATO'S KEEPING WATCH, AND EVERYONE ELSE IS ASLEEP.

WELL ...
I DON'T THINK YUKO IS SLEEPING ...

AND I THINK SATOMI IS UP.

YUKA WAS TOTALLY OUT.
HA HA HA!

...
AND NANAHARA ...
HE STILL ISN'T SHOWING ANY SIGN OF WAKING.

...I SEE...
BUT I KNOW HE'LL BE FINE.
I CARRIED HIM YESTERDAY, DIDN'T I?
I COULD HEAR HIS HEARTBEAT.
I CAN'T REALLY EXPLAIN IT... BUT I KNOW HE'LL BE ALL RIGHT.

YEAH ...

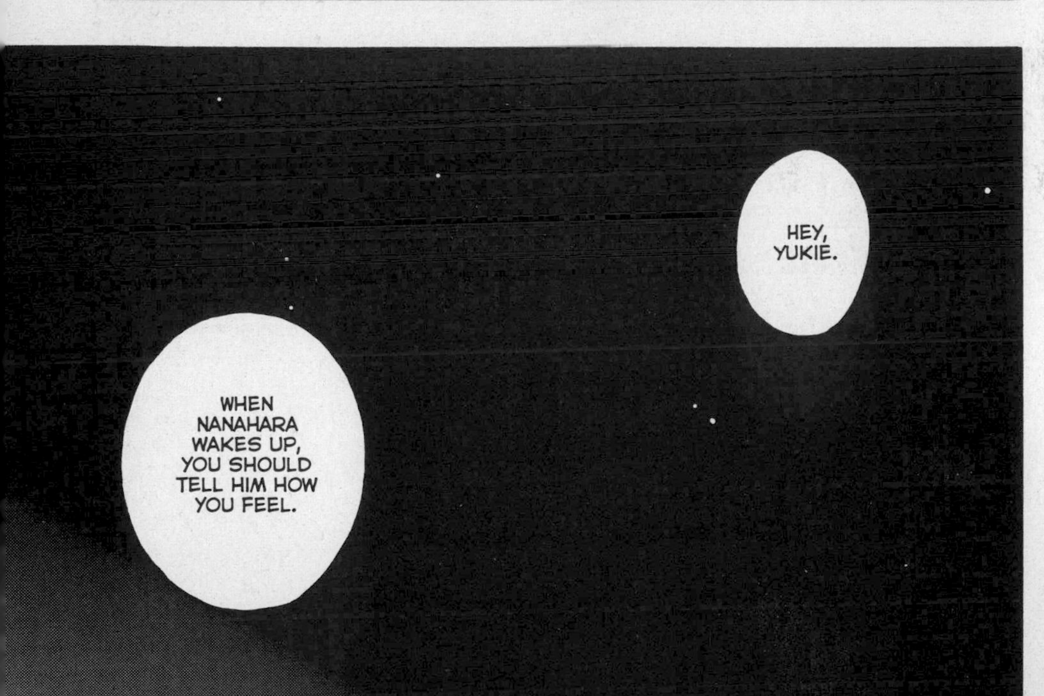
HEY, YUKIE.
WHEN NANAHARA WAKES UP, YOU SHOULD TELL HIM HOW YOU FEEL.

HUH?
OH, COME ON. YOU DON'T NEED TO HIDE IT FROM ME.

DIDN'T YOU JUST SAY THAT I'M YOUR BEST FRIEND?
But...

I suppose I'll keep hiding it from her.
...

I'll hide my feelings for her...
... forever.

SHU

THAT-
YOUR SPEECH YESTERDAY WAS INCREDIBLE ...
IT WAS BECAUSE YOU TRULY WANT TO SAVE HIM, RIGHT?
MY SPEECH ?
YOU KNOW ...
"LET'S SHARE OUR HOPE"?
Actually ...
...Yuko wasn't the only one uneasy about bringing Nanahara in.

But then Yukie said...
WE'RE HERE TOGETHER BECAUSE WE SHARE HOPE.

IF WE REFUSE TO HELP AN INJURED PERSON RIGHT IN FRONT OF OUR EYES...
...THAT HOPE WILL BECOME NOTHING BUT A FRAUD.

AM I WRONG?

MAYBE I WAS JUST BRINGING MY PERSONAL FEELINGS INTO IT.
OTHERWISE, THERE'D BE NO POINT IN US TAKING UP OUR GUNS LIKE SOME BORDER PATROL.

...
I SAID WE WERE LIKE A NATION, RIGHT?

NOT THAT LONG AGO, MY FATHER AND I TALKED ABOUT THIS EXPERIMENT.
REALLY ?!

DID HE TELL YOU ANY-THING?
NO...

HE'S GOT A DESK JOB, SO THIS IS TOTALLY OUT OF HIS FIELD.
SUPPOSING HE DOES KNOW ANYTHING, HE SURELY HAS TO KEEP IT SECRET—EVEN FROM HIS FAMILY.

BUT I KNEW THAT WHEN I WENT INTO NINTH GRADE, THERE WAS A CHANCE I'D BE *CHOSEN*.
SO I HAD TO ASK HIM, JUST ONCE.

"WHAT *IS* THE EXPERIMENT? WHY FORCE JUNIOR HIGH STUDENTS TO KILL EACH OTHER?"
THAT'S WHAT I ASKED HIM.

MY FATHER TOLD ME HE DIDN'T KNOW.
BUT HE DID OFFER HIS *GUESS*...
HIS GUESS?
"SHARED FEAR."

FEAR?
YES.

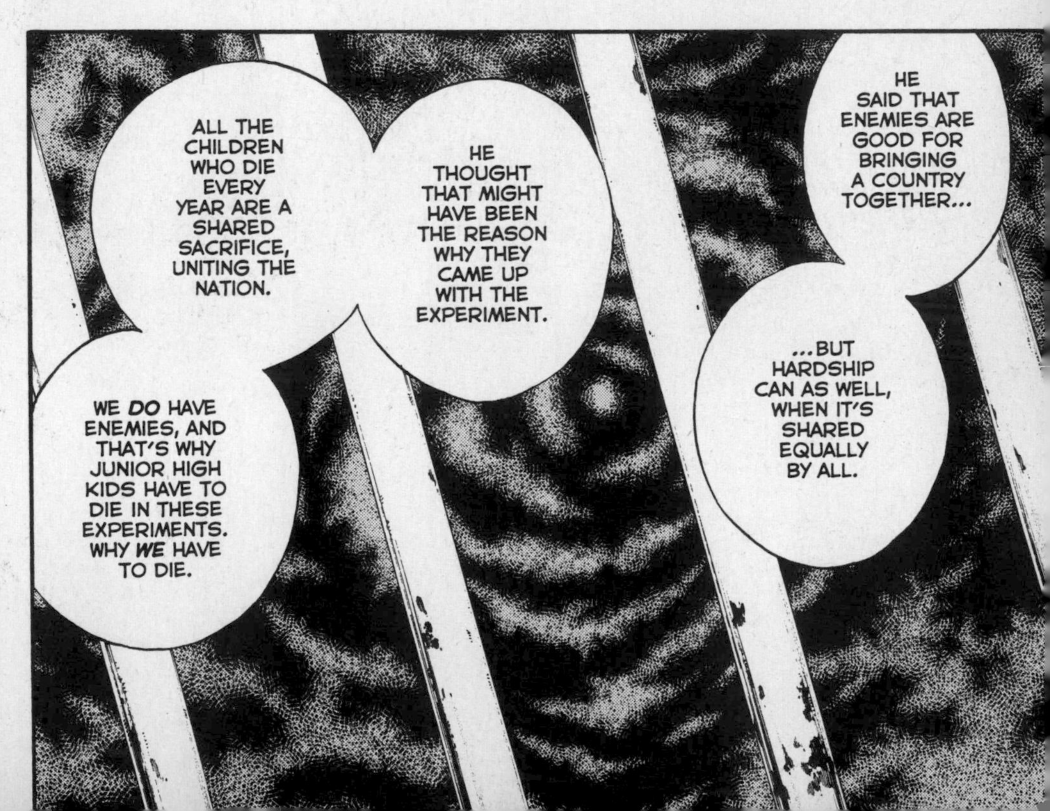
HE SAID THAT ENEMIES ARE GOOD FOR BRINGING A COUNTRY TOGETHER...
...BUT HARDSHIP CAN AS WELL, WHEN IT'S SHARED EQUALLY BY ALL.
HE THOUGHT THAT MIGHT HAVE BEEN THE REASON WHY THEY CAME UP WITH THE EXPERIMENT.
ALL THE CHILDREN WHO DIE EVERY YEAR ARE A SHARED SACRIFICE, UNITING THE NATION.
WE *DO* HAVE ENEMIES, AND THAT'S WHY JUNIOR HIGH KIDS HAVE TO DIE IN THESE EXPERIMENTS. WHY *WE* HAVE TO DIE.

THAT'S ...
THAT'S *STUPID!*

YES. IT'S STUPID.
IF THAT'S WHAT OUR COUNTRY'S LIKE, I DON'T WANT IT.
BUT MY FATHER...

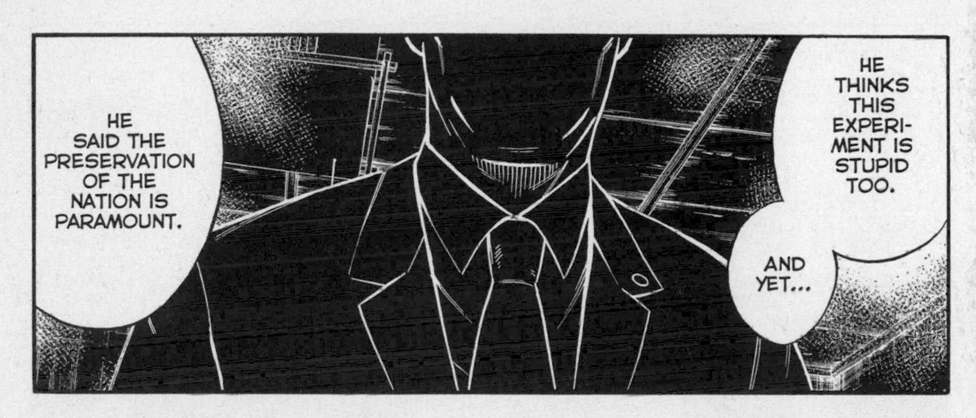
HE THINKS THIS EXPERIMENT IS STUPID TOO.
AND YET...
HE SAID THE PRESERVATION OF THE NATION IS PARAMOUNT.

...
A LITTLE WHILE LATER, HE BOUGHT ME A CELL.

A CELL? LIKE A CELL PHONE?
YEAH.

HE SAID THAT IF ANYTHING HAPPENED, I SHOULD CALL HIM IMMEDIATELY...
...AND HE'D DO WHAT HE COULD TO HELP.
BUT I...

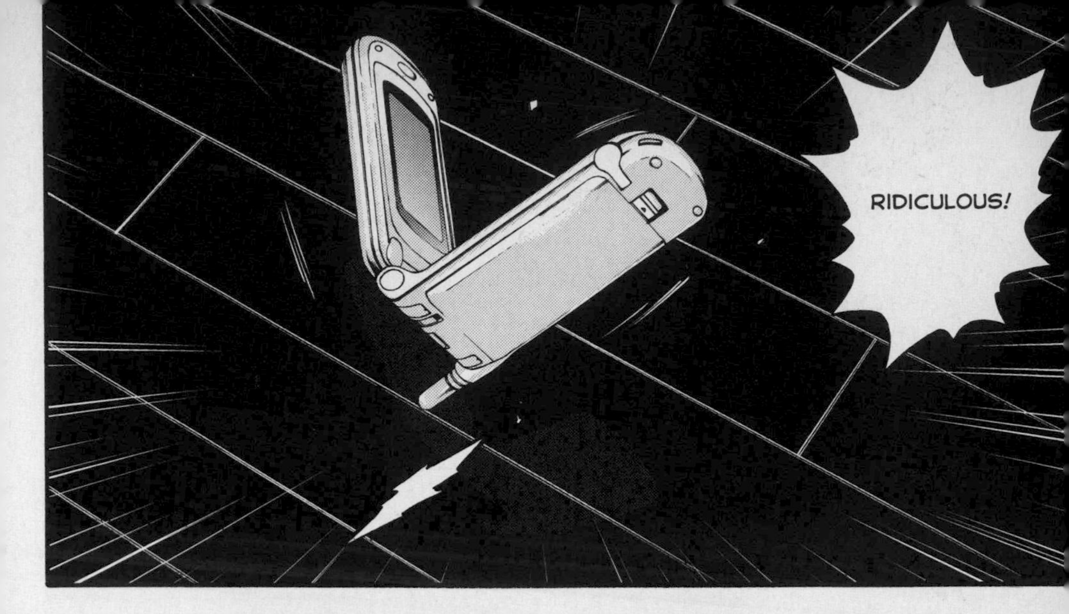
RIDICULOUS!

IF YOUR BELOVED COUNTRY ASKS FOR YOUR DAUGHTER, WHY DON'T YOU JUST *GIVE HER UP?!*
IF THAT'S WHAT YOU WANT, I'LL BE GLAD TO DIE.

... THAT'S WHAT I TOLD HIM.
OF COURSE ...

Yukie...
...EVEN IF I HAD THAT PHONE NOW, I DON'T BELIEVE IT WOULD CHANGE ANYTHING.

She's always so calm and well-mannered, but now...
BUT EVER SINCE...
PHONES WOULDN'T GET RECEPTION OUT HERE, ANYWAY.
EVER SINCE THEN, THINGS BETWEEN US WERE STRAINED.
I NEVER REALLY TALKED TO HIM...

PLIP

WHY... DID I SAY THAT TO HIM?
HE WAS JUST LOOKING AFTER ME THE BEST HE COULD.
NOW I'LL NEVER SEE HIM AGAIN... WHY DID I SAY SUCH A THING?

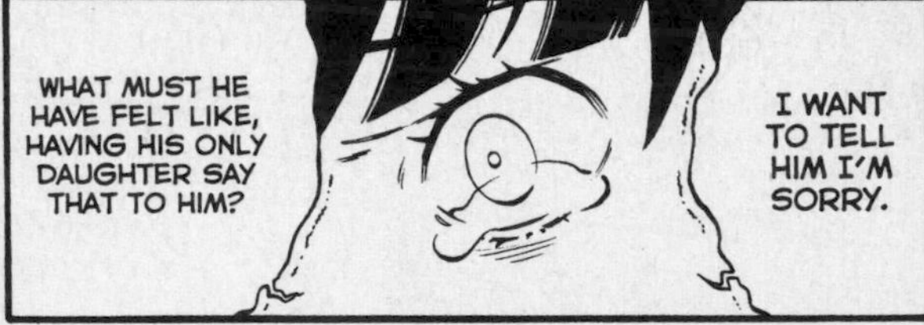
I WANT TO TELL HIM I'M SORRY.
WHAT MUST HE HAVE FELT LIKE, HAVING HIS ONLY DAUGHTER SAY THAT TO HIM?

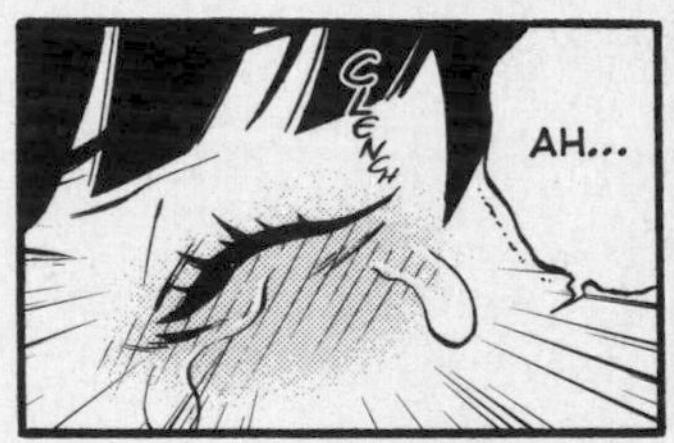
AH...
CLENCH

Dear God...

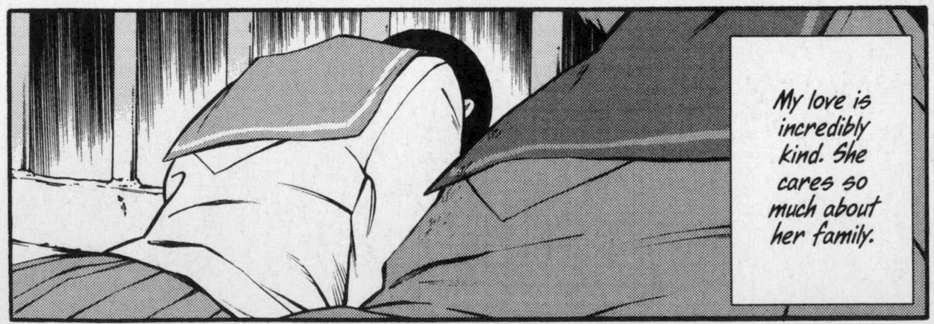
My love is incredibly kind. She cares so much about her family.

And she's crying.

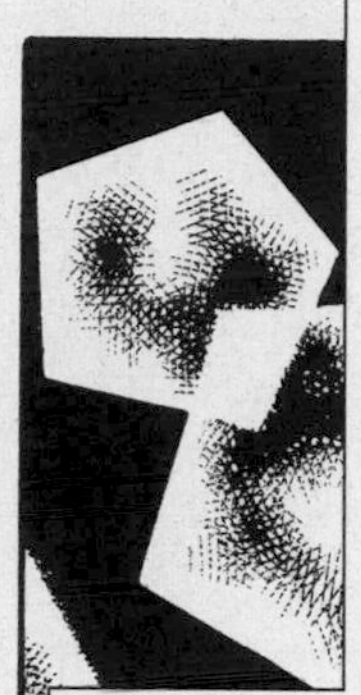
What I'm about to do, I'm not doing out of those kinds of feelings.

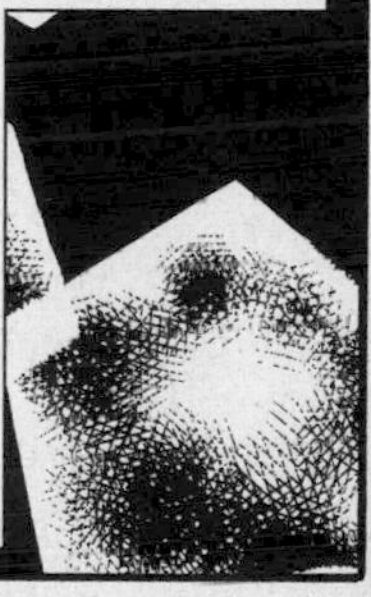
I just want her to feel better.

She's important to me.

This I swear...

And I love her.
HUG
YUKIE!
LET'S MAKE IT TO THE NATIONALS THIS YEAR.

THE NATION-ALS...? THE TOURNA-MENT?
LIKE VOLLEY-BALL?
Oh...
Why is this little thing all I can find to say?
OF COURSE! WE'LL GO WITH THE WHOLE TEAM.
YOU CAN'T GIVE UP NOW.
WE MIGHT STILL HAVE A CHANCE. SOMETHING MIGHT HAPPEN TO CANCEL THIS. MAYBE NANAHARA HAS AN IDEA.

ANYWAY, THE MOMENT YOU GIVE UP, YOU *LOSE*.
IT'S JUST LIKE A VOLLEY-BALL MATCH.
OUR OPPONENTS HAVE TAKEN EVERY POINT AND EVERY SET. IT'S MATCH POINT...
...AND WE HAVEN'T SCORED ONCE. BUT WE CAN'T THINK LIKE WE'VE ALREADY LOST.
WE *CAN'T*!

...but it's the best I can do.
LET'S SHARE OUR HOPE.

OKAY, YUKIE?

... OKAY ...

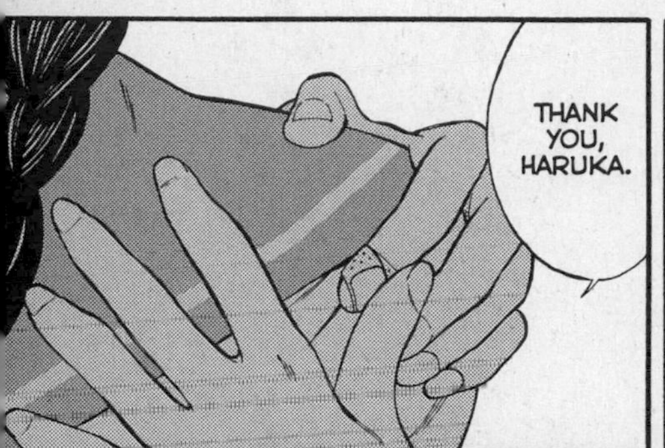
THANK YOU, HARUKA.

THANK YOU...
SHAAAA

MAY 23, 1:11 P.M.
YOU...

EEE ...
YOU'RE DIFFERENT, RIGHT?
EEE ...
RIGHT ?
RIGHT?

BANG

HUFF
HUFF
HUFF
HUFF
HUFF
POP POP POP POP

SHAAA
SHAAA

SHAAA
Hey, Yukie.
Let's share our hope.
SHASHAAA
Okay?
Okay...?
SHAAAA

Battle Royale
Angels' Border
Episode 1......END

Oki Island Map

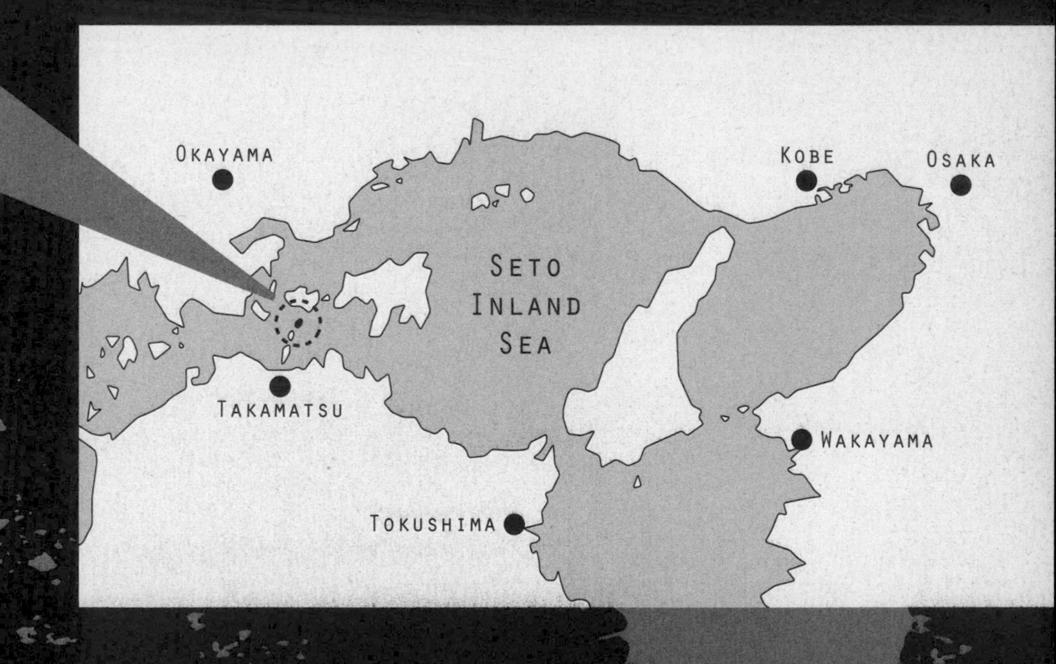

OKI ISLAND

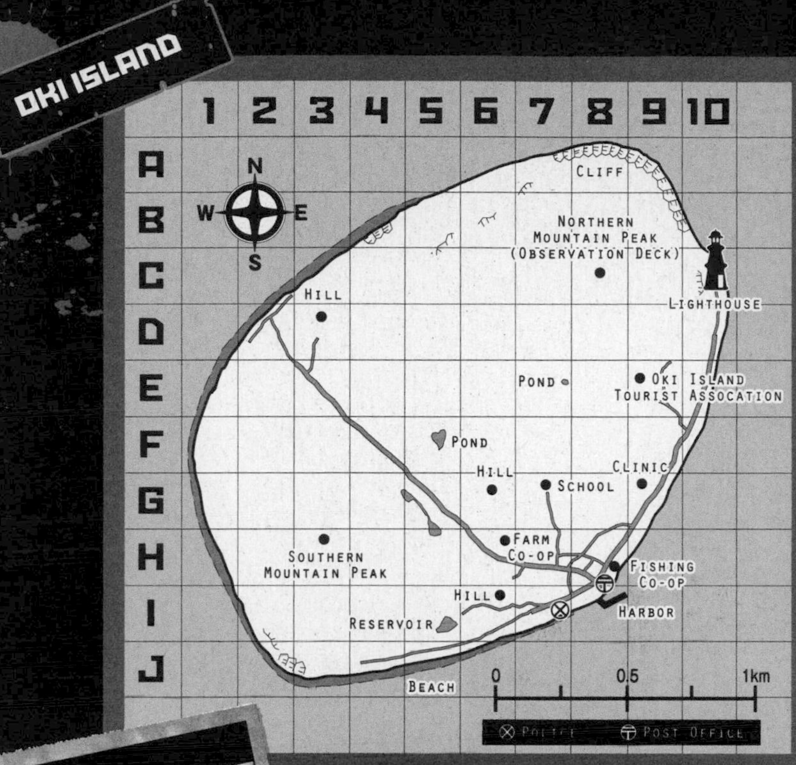

SCHEDULED FORBIDDEN ZONES

22ND		
AM	3:08	G-7
	7:00	J-2
	9:00	F-1
	11:00	H-8
PM	1:00	J-5
	3:00	H-3
	5:00	D-8
	7:00	G-1
	9:00	I-3
	11:00	G-9

23RD		
AM	1:00	F-7
	3:00	G-3
	5:00	E-4
	7:00	C-8
	9:00	D-2
	11:00	C-3
PM	1:00	D-7
	3:00	H-4
	5:00	F-9
	7:00	B-9
	9:00	E-10
	11:00	F-4

Battle Royale: Angels' Border

EPISODE TWO

Art by Oguma Youhei

…Leap for yourself…

EPISODE II

Act 1...Encounter

In this experiment...
...every six hours an announcement...
...lets us know who's died.
I've been good friends with Izumi Kanai...
...since we started junior high.
Her name was in the first announcement.
I don't know where she died.
But I'm fairly sure that...
...someone else in our class...
...killed her.
I know because...
...the main rule of this experiment is...
...that we will kill each other...
...until only one of us is left.

In our country, the Republic of Greater East Asia...
MAY 22, 8:45 P.M.
...all ninth graders are potential subjects...
...for the experiment.
But none of the forty-two students in Shiroiwa Junior High's Ninth Grade Class B...
...ever thought it would happen to us.
Without warning...
...we were taken to a deserted island...
...and given weapons.

The one good thing in this tragedy...
...is that our class leader, Yukie Utsumi...
...assembled the five of us girls here.

Avoiding the fighting, we holed up inside this lighthouse.
We're taking turns keeping watch.
Yuko Sakaki showed up later and we took her in, bringing us up to six.
But we don't have a way to get off the island.
And even worse, the experiment has a time limit, and if we reach it, we all die.
TREMBLE
TREMBLE
For now, we pass time without hope.

Almost a full day has passed since the game began.
According to the 6 P.M. announcement...
...only twenty-one of us remain—exactly half the class.

Whether we hold out here until the time limit expires...
...or whether we don't...
...I know I'll soon be following Izumi.
Oddly enough, I'm not that afraid...
...of death itself.
But...

Shinji Mimura
...I have only one...
...regret.

November, last year.

ATTENTION, PASSENGERS.
THE TRAIN WILL ARRIVE SHORTLY ON TRACK TWO.
RITSURIN
Ritsurin
KITACHO
PLEASE STAND BEHIND THE WHITE LINE.
SIGH...
HOOONK

CLA-
CLACK
CLA-
CLACK
KAWAMOTO
DENTIST

CLA-CLACK
CLA-CLACK
DR RITSURIN

KSHHH
UMM...
OH.
THERE'S AN OPEN SEAT.
TAP
TAP
TAP
HALT
Huh?
It's open, but...
...that guy looks shady.

ANY...
ANY OTHERS?
FWIP FWIP
!

SPRAWL
Him.
Maybe he'll let me sit...
GLANCE

HMPH.
OH.
MAYBE NOT.

DARN.
Guess I'll stand.
...SUI!
!
MATSUI!
?!

Huh?
WHO'S THAT?
SHING
?!
MI-
MIMURA?
THIS ONE'S OPEN.
TAKE A SEAT.

WANT ME TO PUT YOUR BAG ON THE RACK?
NO.
IT'S... NOT THAT HEAVY.
CLUTCH
In my class...
...Eighth Grade, Class B...
...there're forty-one students...
...twenty-one girls and twenty boys.
More than any other boy...
...Mimura has a certain...
...aura.
He's only in eighth grade, but he's a star on the basketball team.
He's way more knowledge-able...
...than our teachers.
And he looks...well, as you can see, pretty cool!
So...
CLENCH
...maybe it's only natural...

...that everyone says...
STARE
...that he's a playboy.
He's only in eighth grade...
...but the other kids debate whether or not...
VAGUE
...he carries a... c-con...
One of those ...
LIGHT HEADED
... rubber things!
THIS ISN'T A SCHOOL DAY...
SO WHAT'S WITH THE UNIFORM?
OH, UH...
NO REASON.
At school ...
...we hardly ever talk.
But he's giving me that smile.
If I hadn't heard what the other girls in Class B say about him...
...I might even...

I might even...
...get taken in by it...
...and smile back.
!
TAP
TAP
...
TAP

What?
That guy...
He's pretending not to notice!
EXCUSE ME, MA'AM—
MA'AM!
SHUP
?!

PLEASE, HAVE MY SEAT.
...
BOW
THANK YOU. THAT'S VERY NICE OF YOU.
OH, IT'S NOTHING.
...
THE TRAIN IS ABOUT...
...TO DEPART...
What a creep.
Why...
...is he being like-
DON'T LOOK.
WHAT?

LET HIM BE.
MEDDLE WITH STUPID AND YOU'LL CATCH IT.
SOMEONE ONCE WROTE...
...
..."EVIL IS JUST A MATTER OF STUPIDITY."
THAT'S TRUE ON MANY LEVELS, BUT...
...IN THIS CASE-
GRAB
YA
NK
?!
BY "STUPID," DID YOU MEAN ME?
OH?
YOU HEARD?

I'M BETTER THAN SOME OLD WOMAN ...
...DRAWING HER PENSION CHECK SO SHE CAN BUY NICE CLOTHES!
GRAB
I WAS WORKING ALL NIGHT! I'M TIRED.
AND YOU, YOU'RE A STUDENT, YEAH?
DON'T GIVE ME THAT LOOK, LIKE YOU'RE BETTER THAN ME...
...WHEN YOU'RE LIVING OFF YOUR *PARENTS'* MONEY.
!
...

I'M SORRY...
WHAT WAS THAT?
I DIDN'T MEAN IT.
WHAT DO YOU MEAN, YOU DIDN'T MEAN IT?!
YOU...
YOU THINK I'M A JOKE? I'LL FUCKING KILL YOU!
THAT'S RIGHT.
SHOVE
YOU BETTER WATCH YOURSELF.
HMPH.
FWUMP
SILENCE
THE NEXT STOP IS KITACHO.
KITACHO.
MATSUI.

SORRY TO ASK YOU THIS...
CREAK
WOULD YOU GET OFF WITH ME AT THE NEXT STOP?

WHAT?
SHOCK
THERE'S A REASON.

PLEASE TRUST ME.

OH...
OKAY.
Well... if I stay on the train, it'll be awkward now anyway, right?

I can just wait for the next train...
RSHHH
NOW ARRIVING IN KITACHO.
THIS IS KITACHO.
OKAY, LET'S GO.
GLANCE
BOW
NOW...

LET'S ESCAPE.
ESCAPE?
HEY ...
UH...
WHA-?
TROMP TROMP

At least... that's the story.

THIS MONTH, THEY'RE DOING AN "IMPROVE PUBLIC MANNERS" DRIVE.

LIKELY AT THE NEXT STOP OR SO, A CROWD OF THE YOUTH CORPS WILL RUSH ONTO THE TRAIN.

THEY'LL GIVE THAT GUY A TALKING-TO.

THERE MIGHT EVEN BE POLICE...

HE MIGHT GET DETAINED.

I SAW HIM ON THE RADIO.
OH... SO...
WHY DO *WE* HAVE TO ESCAPE?
...
WELL, IT TAKES TWO SIDES TO QUARREL. THEY MIGHT DECIDE TO QUESTION US.
I DON'T WANT THAT.
AND...
...TODAY, THERE'RE CERTAIN FACTORS ...
...THAT MEAN THE POLICE ARE TROUBLE FOR ME.
Factors?

LEAVING YOU BEHIND...
...WOULD REVEAL MY IDENTITY.
I'M SORRY, BUT...

SWISH
...PLEASE COME WITH ME FOR A LITTLE WHILE.
WE'LL TRANSFER TO THE KOTOHIRA LINE...
...AND TAKE A BUS BACK TO SHIROIWA.
THAT WON'T BE A PROBLEM, WIIL IT?

WHAT'S WRONG?
...
YOU DON'T TRUST ME? BECAUSE OF MY BAD REPUTATION?

DON'T WORRY.

I NEVER HIT ON GIRLS...
...WITH LESS THAN A C-CUP.
URK!

I PROMISE.
I WON'T DO ANYTHING FUNNY. I WON'T THINK ANYTHING FUNNY.

...
SIGH...

SCREECH
TAXI
I...
...DON'T HAVE THE ALLOW-ANCE...
...TO PAY FOR A TAXI.

I'LL PAY, OF COURSE.
AND THE BUS AND TRAIN FARE TOO.
DON'T WORRY ABOUT A THING!

MAY 22, 2:40 A.M.
NEXT IS GIRL NUMBER NINETEEN, CHISATO MATSUI.
EEP!
?!
CHISATO!

WHIRL
...
CHISATO!
HURRY!
!!
YU-
SOB
YUKIE
...
YUKIE!
EVERY-
ONE!

SHHH.
DON'T SHOUT.
THE NEXT ONE'LL COME SOON.
OH, SORRY.
BUT THE NEXT IS...
WAIT...
IS THIS ALL OF YOU?

...YEAH.

OH.... DID YOU SEE...
...MIMURA COME OUT?

HMM? MIMURA WENT OFF SOME-WHERE.
WHY?

But...
He...

NEXT.
BOY NUMBER NINETEEN, SHINJI MIMURA.
CLATTER
MAY 22, 2:37 A.M.

SHFF
MIMURA ...
THERE HE GOES...
SHFF
SHFF
SHU
Mimura!
CLENCH

SHAAAA

EPISODE II
Act 2...Part
TAXI
UMM...
TAKE U TO MATSU-SHIMA SANCHO STATION.
... KOTOHIRA LINE, PLEASE.
NOD
VRROOM
THERE.
IF YOU TURN THERE, IT'S FASTER.
THAT SHOUL TAKE YO STRAIGH TO THE HIGHWA
YEAH, IT DOES.
YOU KNOW A LOT, MISTER.
ARE YOU A POLICE DETECTIVE?
TURN
AND SHE'S YOUR PRISONER?

IF I WERE A DETECTIVE, I WOULDN'T BE CATCHING A TRAIN.
I'D HAVE YOU TAKE US TO THE PREFECTURAL HQ.
...RIGHT.
BUT STILL...
...YOU HAVE THAT LOOK ABOUT YOU.

WHAT?
NO, NOT US.
...

THANKS.
VROOM
MATSUSHIMA SANCHOME STATION
TAXI

HE CALLED ME A DETECTIVE...
ME.
DO I LOOK THAT OLD?
DO YOU THINK IT'S MY SUNGLASSES?
RESTAURANT
Kreen House
in
MAYBE.
BUT CALLING YOU A PRISONER WAS PRETTY HARSH.
...
I THINK... MAYBE...
...IT'S BECAUSE I SEEM SO DRAB.
SHK
REALLY?
I DON'T THINK THAT'S TRUE AT ALL.
YOU'RE REALLY CUTE...
...MATSUI.

So...
AND... AND THEN ...
WE'LL GET OFF AT SHIDO, THEN TAKE A BUS?
RIGHT. LET'S LOOK AT THE TRAIN SCHEDULE.
That's how he does it. With a casual compliment.
WATCH OUT.
WATCH OUT.
Actually ...
...I did meet with a detective because of my brother.
SIGH...
...

HMMM... LOOKS LIKE WE JUST MISSED IT.
STOP !!

THERE'LL BE ANOTHER IN TWENTY MINUTES.
Jump?
?
You want me to jump?
No, er...
...

YOU WANT TO SIT?
NO.
LET'S DUCK INTO THE RESTAU-RANT OVER THERE.

YOU DON'T HAVE TO.
IT'S FINE, IT'S FINE.
FRANKLY, I'M GETTING COLD OUT HERE.
ALL RIGHT, BUT I CAN PAY FOR-
IT'S FINE, IT'S FINE.

I'VE PUT YOU THROUGH ALL THIS TROUBLE.
LET ME BUY YOU SOME-THING.
HUH?

HAVE YOU HEARD OF SHAREWARE?

WWW:
Digital Camera Softwar
anking
AlbumMaker 1.0
ImageAssassin 3.0
JAlbum 1-Click Ima
IT SOUNDS FAMILIAR...
ARE THOSE THE PROGRAMS PEOPLE PUT ON THE NET...
...AND SELL TO OTHER PEOPLE?
YEAH. I'VE EARNED SOME MONEY...
...DOING THAT.
SO DON'T WORRY ABOUT IT.
...
THAT'S AMAZING! YOU CAN MAKE STUFF LIKE THAT?
NO...
MY BIGGEST SELLER IS BUILT ON SOMETHING MY UNCLE CREATED.
ALL I DID WAS TWEAK IT A LITTLE.
IS THAT YOUR UNCLE'S JOB?
NO...
...?
S-SO, THAT GUY ON THE TRAIN... WHAT A JERK, RIGHT?
Kreen House
YEAH.

TIRED FROM HIS ALL-NIGHTER, WAS HE?
HE WAS TAKING UP TWO SEATS.
AND THAT OLD WOMAN...
ANYONE COULD SEE SHE HAD WEAK LEGS.
WELL, ABOUT NOW HE'S PROBABLY SUR-ROUNDED BY THE YOUTH CORPS...
...GETTING TOLD A THING OR TWO.
GRIP
BUT HONESTLY...
I LIKE THE YOUTH CORPS EVEN LESS.
CHAK
Children under 18 are not permitted to enter these premises after 6:00 P.M.
SMILE
WELCOME.
JINGLE
JINGLE
HAVING MANNERS... AND BY THAT I MEAN BEING KIND TO OTHERS...

...IS A GOOD THING.
BUT IF YOU DON'T UNDERSTAND THE BEAUTY OF VIRTUE...
...GOOD MANNERS ARE AN EMPTY GESTURE.
...
TABLE FOR TWO?
WILL YOU BE SMOKING TODAY?

NO, I QUIT.
HOW ABOUT YOU?
"I quit"?
OF COURSE NOT.
I'M IN MY SCHOOL UNIFORM. JUNIOR HIGH SCHOOL.
THIS WAY, PLEASE.
ORDER WHATEVER YOU LIKE.
FALL DESSERTS
Mont Blanc Tart 580 yen
Seasonal Fruit Macedonia 720 yen with Panna Cotta
Autumn Fig Tart 600yen
Drink Menu
Hot Coffee
Iced Coffee
Café Au Lait
Espresso
Hot Cocoa
ALL 280円

I'M GOOD WITH TEA. MILK TEA.
TMP
ARE YOU SURE?
YOU CAN REALLY HAVE WHATEVER YOU WANT.
MENU

BEEP
NO, THAT'S ALL RIGHT.
REALLY?
OKAY...

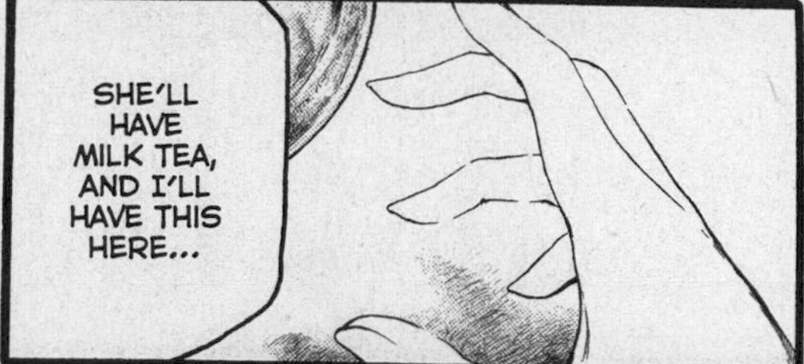
SHE'LL HAVE MILK TEA, AND I'LL HAVE THIS HERE...

...THE FRUIT TAKOYAKI PARFAIT.
WHAT?!

WELL...
I LIKE TAKOYAKI SAUCE.
GRIN

OH...
HUH...
SIP

VRROOM
MENU

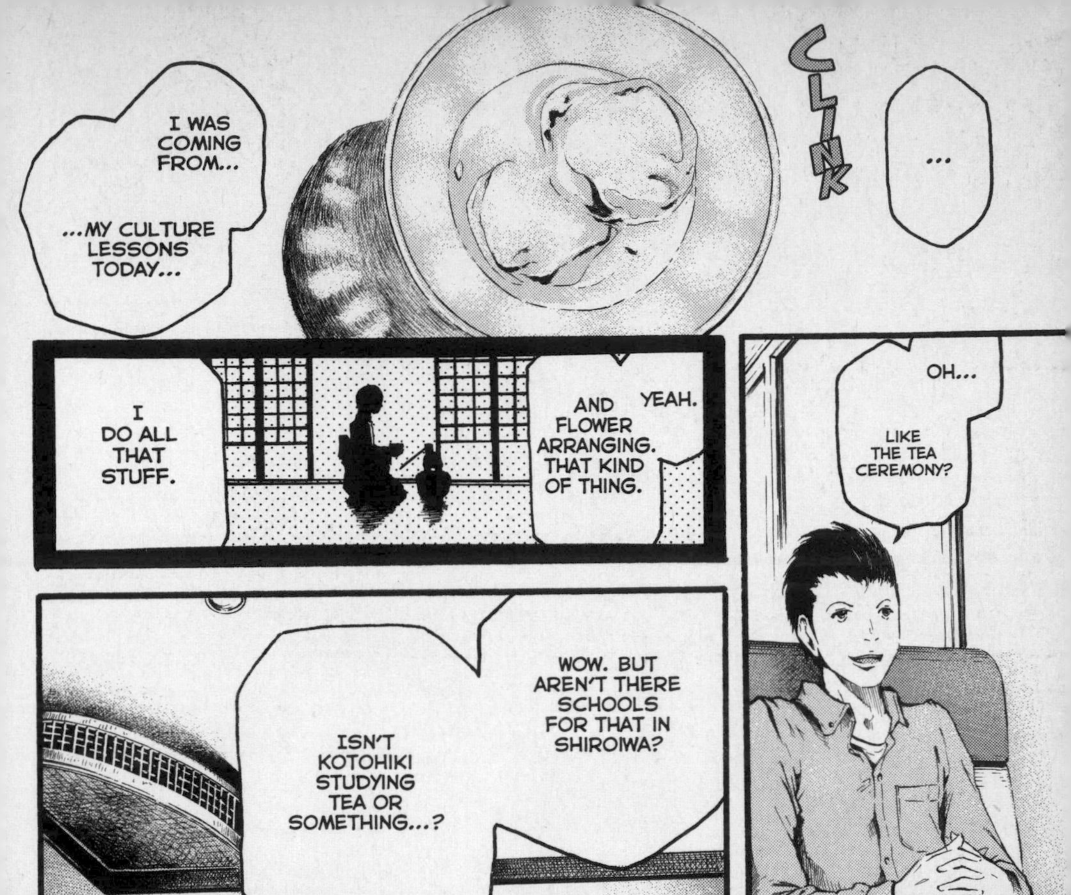
...
CLINK
I WAS COMING FROM...
...MY CULTURE LESSONS TODAY...
OH...
LIKE THE TEA CEREMONY?
YEAH.
AND FLOWER ARRANGING. THAT KIND OF THING.
I DO ALL THAT STUFF.
WOW. BUT AREN'T THERE SCHOOLS FOR THAT IN SHIROIWA?
ISN'T KOTOHIKI STUDYING TEA OR SOMETHING...?

He knows a lot.
OF COURSE HE DOES...
IF IT'S ABOUT GIRLS.
ANYWAY, THE PLACE I GO...
...IS HOSTED BY THE REPUBLIC'S NONAGGRES-SIVE FORCES WIVES ASSOCIATION ...
!
WHAT IS IT?
NOTH-ING.

YOU'VE HEARD OF IT?
YEAH...
YOU'RE ONE OF THOSE TYPES?
LOOK, I DIDN'T MEAN–
IT'S NOT LIKE THAT.
I'M NOT...
...INTO POLITICS OR ANYTHING.

I JUST GO BECAUSE MY PARENTS MAKE ME.
BECAUSE I HAVE TO.

BUT...
CLUTCH
BUT...
TAKING THE LESSONS ISN'T ALL BAD.

I AGREE WITH THE WAY YOU THINK, MIMURA.
MANNERS AREN'T SOMETHING YOU FORCE ON OTHERS.

IT LOOKS GOOD ON YOUR TRAN-SCRIPT?
WELL, THAT TOO, BUT...
...IF I DO REALLY WELL, I CAN BECOME A CULTURAL AMBASSADOR...
...AND MAYBE GO *OUTSIDE* THE COUNTRY.
WOW, THAT *IS* SOMETHING.
In the Republic of Greater East Asia overseas travel...
...is strictly...
...regulated.
The government doesn't think well of "incorrect" foreign information and culture.

I WANT TO SEE OTHER COUNTRIES.
I WANT TO SEE THE MANY DIFFERENT WORLDS OUT THERE.

THAT'S WHY...
...YOU STUDY ENGLISH SO HARD.
WHAT? HOW DID YOU...?
He noticed?
SO...
MY ACCENT...
...ISN'T EVEN THAT GOOD OR ANYTHING.
BUT YOU'RE ALWAYS USING THAT NICE DICTIONARY IN CLASS.
AND YOU LISTEN SO INTENTLY TO THE TEACHER.
ANYONE LOOKING COULD SEE THAT.
Does that mean he's looking?
BUT YOU'RE GOOD AT ENGLISH YOURSELF.
AREN'T YOU INTERESTED IN GOING TO ANOTHER COUNTRY?
BEYOND WHAT I NEED FOR MY CODING...
...I'M PRETTY CLUELESS.
AS FOR FOREIGN COUNTRIES...
OF-
OF COURSE I DON'T THINK...
...THAT OTHER COUNTRIES ARE BETTER THAN THIS ONE, BUT...
...
IS IT A GOOD COUNTRY WHEN...
...YOU'RE OBLI-GATED TO MAKE EXCUSES FOR IT?
!

WELL...
THAT'S ENOUGH HEAVY TALK.
YOU KNOW, IF I MAKE THE NATIONAL TEAM...
...I MIGHT BE ABLE TO GO OUT OF THE COUNTRY TOO.
IF WE GO TO THE SAME PLACE...
LIKE IN A PARISIAN CAFE...
...THEN MAYBE WE COULD SHARE SOME TEA LIKE THIS AGAIN.
I HAVE YOUR ORDER.
MILK TEA AND...
CLINK
...A FRUIT TAKOYAKI PARFAIT.
TAH
DAH
IS THAT EVERY-THING?
UM...
YES?
THAT BOY...
...

...OVER THERE.
HE'S BEEN ALONE...
...THIS WHOLE TIME.
WHERE'S HIS MOTHER? IS HE ALL RIGHT?
...I FEEL KIND OF BAD FOR THE KID.
A LOT OF CHILDREN HAVE BEEN COMING IN BY THEMSELVES LATELY.
HE'S A REGULAR. VERY SMART TOO.
HE'S ALREADY FINISHED HIS MEAL... NOW, IS THERE ANYTHING ELSE?
?
OH.
WHOOSH
?!

BANG
BANG

SMIRK

GRIN

WATCH OUT... HE COULD BE SECRET POLICE...
...EAVES-DROPPING ON OUR CONVERSA-TION.

GIGGLE
COULD BE.

MAY 22, 2:42 A.M.
NO BOYS!
WE ALL DECIDED THAT TOGETHER.

BUT COME ON, WHEN NORIKO WAS SHOT...
...MIMURA TRIED...
...TO HELP HER.

HE TOLD THAT SAKA-MOCHI GUY...
...THAT BECAUSE NORIKO WAS HURT, WE SHOULD POSTPONE–
THAT COULD'VE BEEN AN ACT...
...JUST TO GET US TO TRUST HIM.

SHUSH! THE NEXT BOY'S COMING.
Motobuchi.
!

EEK!

AHHHH-!

RUSTLE
RUSTLE
RUSTLE
...

TMP
?!

THERE'S NOTHING YOU CAN DO.
YUKA...

KATSU— YOU KNOW, KATSU HATAGAMI?
HE CAME OUT A LITTLE BIT AGO...
WE'RE NEIGHBORS, AND WE WERE FRIENDS WHEN WE WERE LITTLE.

RUSTLE

RUSTLE
WHA?
CHK
YUKIE-SHOULD WE SHOOT?
WAIT!

Oh...
Mimura, is this what I think it is?
That you were really waiting for me?
And...then you realized that the way things are, Yukie and the girls won't accept you.
That's what you're thinking, isn't it?
And so...

And so...
...this is goodbye.
WHAT'S THAT ABOUT?
...AH...
Is that what this is?

Episode II
Act 3...Pray
Kreen House
RESTAURANT Kreen House
Kreen House
OH, LOOK!

OH-
UM...
IF IT ISN'T MIMURA!
LONG TIME NO SEE.
I WAS JUST THINKING ABOUT CALLING YOU.
Who's that guy?
Her boyfriend?
...

OH, THIS IS CHISATO MATSUI.
SHE'S IN MY CLASS.
WE'RE ON THE HEALTH COMMITTEE. OUR TEACHER'S INJURED, SO WE'RE PAYING HIM A VISIT.
Representing the class.
OH ...
SO *THAT'S* IT.
?
BOWS
I THOUGHT SHE MIGHT HAVE BEEN...
...THE LITTLE SISTER YOU MEN-TIONED.
'CAUSE SHE'S SO TINY.
Thanks for re-minding me.
WHAT?!
I'M...
...KANA HOTTA.
I PLAY BASKETBALL AT TAKAMATSU VOCATIONAL.
NICE TO MEET YOU.
OUR TEACHER RUPTURED HIS ACHILLES TENDON.
HE'S ONE OF THE BADMINTON COACHES...
...SO THE TEAM'S COMING TO MEET US.
WE'RE WAITING FOR THEM NOW.
Well, he's a smooth liar.

OH, OKAY.
WELL ...
SORRY FOR BUTTING IN.
IT'S TOO BAD YOU'RE NOT HIS SISTER ...
I COULD HAVE ASKED YOUR ADVICE ABOUT MY FUTURE.
YOUR FUTURE ?
GLANCE
LIKE, TOTALLY.
HE AND I MIGHT GET MARRIED SOMEDAY.
OKAY.
I'LL BE CALLING YOU FOR SURE!
THIS YEAR HE WAS THE MVP AT THE...
...JUNIOR HIGH PREFECTURAL TOURNAMENT.
NO WAY!
SO HE'S IN *JUNIOR HIGH*?
CHATTER
CHATTER
JAILBAIT, HUH?
BUT HE *IS* COOL!
...
HER CHEST SEEMS BIG ENOUGH.
WHAT ?!

NO, NO.
I KNOW HOW THAT MUST HAVE SOUNDED...
...BUT I HAVEN'T DONE ANYTHING WITH *HER* YET.
"Yet," huh?
"Her," huh?
BUT...
WELL...
I'M NOT SURE IF WE'RE EXACTLY DATING OR NOT...
ANYWAY, EXPLAINING WOULD'VE BEEN A HASSLE.
...YOU'RE DATING HER...
...AND YOU *LIED* TO HER.
WHAT WAS THAT ABOUT US VISITING OUR TEACHER?
WITH EVERYTHING THAT HAPPENED TODAY AND ALL...
IT MAY NOT SEEM LIKE IT, BUT SHE'S BEEN THROUGH A LOT. HER PARENTS' DIVORCE, FOR ONE.
WHEN WE WERE IN THE SEVENTH TO TWELFTH GRADE PREFECTURE-WIDE ATHLETIC CAMP...
...SHE CAME TO ME FOR ADVICE.

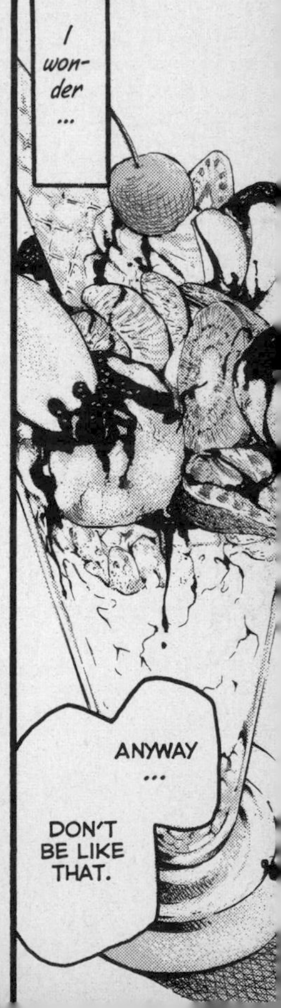
I wonder...
ANYWAY...
DON'T BE LIKE THAT.

A HIGH SCHOOLER COMING TO SOME-ONE...
...IN JUNIOR HIGH FOR ADVICE?

HEY...
...IT HAPPENS.
Ooh, hot...

...
DON'T THINK TOO BADLY OF HER.
HUH?
WHAT DO YOU MEAN?
YOU KNOW, HOW SHE SAID...
...YOU WERE TINY.
...
SHE...

...DOESN'T...
...SEEM TO LIKE BEING TALL.
SO WHEN SHE SAID YOU WERE TINY...
...SHE DIDN'T MEAN ANYTHING BY IT...I DON'T THINK.
CLINK
WHAT ABOUT YOU, MIMURA?
YOU DON'T SEEM TO HAVE ANY HANG-UPS.
...

DON'T I?
WELL, YOU'RE GOOD AT SPORTS AND YOU GET GOOD GRADES.
AND YOU'RE POPULAR WITH GIRLS.
AND-
WHAT?
GRAB
EVERY DAY...
...BEFORE I GET OUT OF BED...
...I PRAY.
YOU PRAY?
REALLY?
WELL... ONLY FOR A COUPLE OF MINUTES, BUT...

...I ASK FOR NOTHING BAD TO HAPPEN THAT DAY.
THEN I FINALLY GET UP.
UMM... SO... DO YOU...
WELL... BELIEVE IN GOD?
NO. BUT...
IT'S LIKE...
YOU KNOW HOW MUSLIMS ARE ALWAYS PRAYING?
I THINK I WAS JUST BORN THE TYPE OF PERSON ...
...WHO SUITS THAT LIFE-STYLE.
BUT EVEN SO... ...I HATE RELIGION, OF COURSE.
I THINK ANYONE WHO CLAIMS THEY KNOW WHAT GOD IS LIKE IS A FOOL.
AND YET I CAN'T HELP BUT PRAY.
PRETTY SAD, RIGHT?

...DID SOMETHING BAD HAPPEN TO YOU?
WELL...
AFTER I STARTED SPENDING A LOT OF TIME WITH MY UNCLE...
...HE TAUGHT ME EVERYTHING, EVEN BASKETBALL.
I FORGOT THAT THE WORLD WAS SUCH A FRIGHTENING PLACE.
BUT EVEN NOW, I CAN'T STOP.
IN THE MORNING, I PRAY.
CLINK
PLEASE DON'T TELL ANYONE.
NO ONE KNOWS BUT YUTAKA...
SETO, I MEAN.
I HAVEN'T EVEN TOLD NANAHARA.
...
I THINK ONE REASON I DO IT IS...
...JUST MAYBE...

...WHEN I WAS LITTLE...
... SOMEONE ONCE SAID TO ME...
...THAT SOME OF MY ANCESTORS- DISTANT ONES, BUT STILL...
...DID SOMETHING BAD THAT MADE THEM RICH.
AND THAT THEIR WICKED BLOOD RUNS INSIDE ME.
I KNOW IT'S NOT A BIG DEAL, BUT-
IT *IS* A BIG DEAL!
WHO SAID THAT TO YOU?

YOU THINK SO?
WELL... I GUESS YUTAKA WAS FURIOUS WHEN I TOLD HIM TOO...
...
SO YOU HAVE A LITTLE SISTER?

YEAH. THREE YEARS YOUNGER. HER NAME'S IKUMI.
SHE'S A REAL SMART-ASS.
WHAT ABOUT YOU? DO YOU HAVE ANY SIBLINGS?
YEAH...
AN OLDER BROTHER.
OH YEAH? I GUESS THAT MAKES US...
...ON THE OPPOSITE END OF THINGS.
WHAT'S YOUR BROTHER DOING? IS HE IN OUR SCHOOL? IN HIGH SCHOOL?
WELL... I WAS BORN...
...A BIT AFTER HIM.
CLINK
SO, COLLEGE?
NUH UH
IS HE STILL TRYING TO GET INTO A COLLEGE?
HE WAS.
WAS? WHAT ABOUT NOW?
SIGH...
Kreen House
Kreen House
HE DIED LAST YEAR.
HE KILLED HIMSELF.

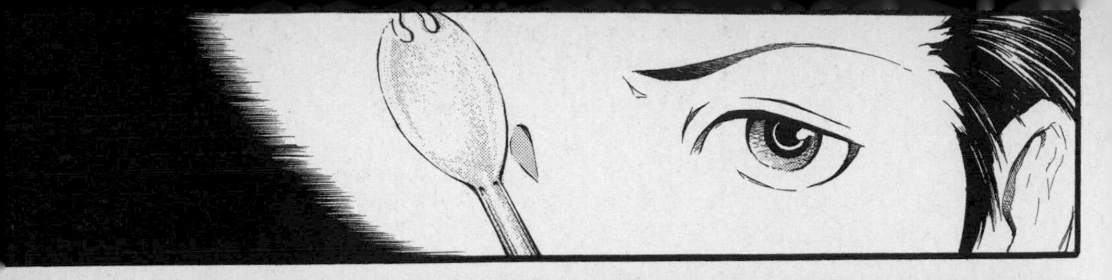

MAY 23, 12:24 A.M.

BRAT TAT TAT TAT TAT TAT

UNCLE...
MATSU...
...I...
IKUMI...

SORRY. I DIDN'T KNOW.

NO...
IT'S OKAY.

WE WERE IN DIFFERENT CLASSES LAST YEAR.
AND IT'S A LITTLE DIFFERENT THAN IF MY PARENTS HAD DIED.

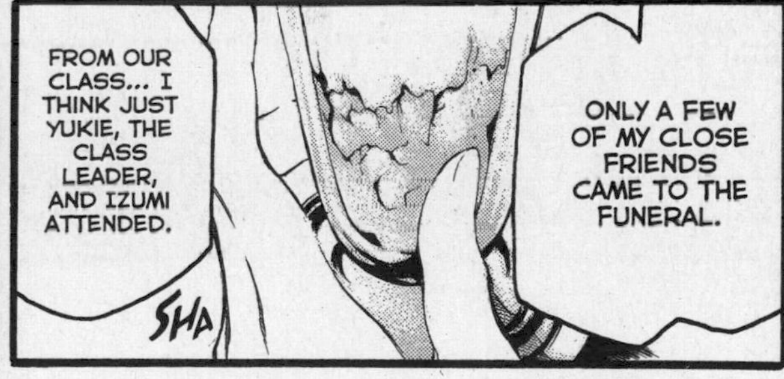

ONLY A FEW OF MY CLOSE FRIENDS CAME TO THE FUNERAL.
FROM OUR CLASS... I THINK JUST YUKIE, THE CLASS LEADER, AND IZUMI ATTENDED.
SHA

EXCUSE ME.
COULD I GET A COFFEE PLEASE?

AFTER MY BROTHER FAILED THE COLLEGE ENTRANCE EXAM...
...HE GOT INVOLVED IN SOME... THINGS...

DO YOU KNOW ABOUT ANTI-GOVERNMENT GROUPS?
SURE, I GUESS...

NOW...
I DON'T KNOW WHAT REALLY HAPPENED.

BUT THE POLICE CAME AND TOOK HIM IN FOR QUESTIONING...
EVEN AFTER HE WAS RELEASED, I NEVER TALKED TO HIM ABOUT IT.
AND OF COURSE I NEVER BROUGHT IT UP WITH MY FATHER OR MY MOTHER.

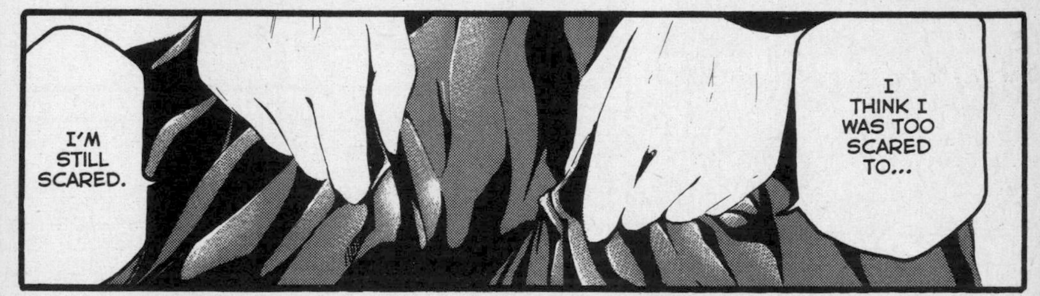
I THINK I WAS TOO SCARED TO...
I'M STILL SCARED.

BUT...
SINCE HE WAS RELEASED...
...HE CAN'T HAVE BEEN INVOLVED.

IF HE HAD BEEN...
...EVEN AS A MINOR, HE WOULDN'T HAVE BEEN LET OUT FOR AT LEAST SIX MONTHS.

YOU KNOW A LOT.
THE DETECTIVE TOLD ME THE SAME THING.
AFTER MY BROTHER CAME BACK...
...I DON'T KNOW IF I'D CALL HIM A RECLUSE, EXACTLY, BUT...
...HE KIND OF BECAME A HERMIT.
I GUESS.
I CERTAINLY DON'T THINK HE GAVE UP ON PASSING THE EXAMS.
HE WAS STILL BUYING COLEGE PREP BOOKS.
UH-HUH.
BUT...
IN THE END, HE WENT OFF ON HIS OWN...
...WITHOUT TELLING ANY OF US.
HE ONLY LEFT A SIMPLE NOTE.

OH...
YEAH.

I THINK THAT'S WHY MY PARENTS ...
...MADE ME START TAKING LESSONS FROM THE NON-AGGRESSIVE FORCES WIVES ASSOCIATION.
Ettiquette School
Master the proper manners of the

THEY NEVER REALLY TOLD ME WHY.
AND I NEVER ASKED, BUT...
SIGH...
THAT'S THE ONLY EXPLANATION, ISN'T IT?

I THINK IT WAS A WAY FOR THEM TO ANNOUNCE THAT...
...THIS GIRL'S BEHAVIOR IS PURE AND PROPER.
SHE'S STUDYING THE IDEALS OF THIS GREAT NATION.
SHE HAS ABSOLUTELY NO CONNECTION WHATSOEVER TO ANY ANTI-GOVERNMENT MOVEMENT.

UH-HUH.
I DON'T MIND TEA AND FLOWERS ON THEIR OWN.
I RATHER LIKE THEM, ACTUALLY.
I COULD MAYBE DO WITHOUT RECITING THE LEADER'S ANALECTS, BUT...
...WE HAVE TO DO THAT AT SCHOOL TOO, ANYWAY.

BUT THEN TODAY ...
... SOMEONE SAID SOMETHING TO ME.

THEY SAID THEY HEARD...
...THAT MY BROTHER WAS INTERROGATED BY THE POLICE.
AFTER ALL...
...SHIROIWA'S NOT SO FAR FROM HERE.
WORD MUST HAVE GOTTEN OUT.
THAT'S COLD.
WHAT'S THE POINT IN BRINGING THAT UP?
THANKS.
SORRY. ALL I'M DOING IS COMPLAINING.
COMPLAIN AWAY.
IF YOU CAN MAKE DO WITH ME, I'LL LISTEN FOR A MILLION HOURS.
A MILLION HOURS?
YEAH.
I'LL LISTEN FOREVER.

...

...WHAT?
YOU CAN'T DO THAT.
MIMURA...
DON'T YOU HAVE TO GO ON A DATE WITH HOTTA?
EH?
AH, WELL...
YEAH, BUT...
HA HA.
OH-

WHAT IS IT?
I THINK THAT BOY'S MOM IS HERE.

TAK
TAK
GOOD.

HALT

YOU'RE NOT GOING TO VISIT YOUR TEACHER.
YOU'RE ON A *DATE*, RIGHT?

BINGO.
IF WE SEE EACH OTHER AGAIN, AND YOU'RE NOT BUSY, YOU WANNA PLAY BASKETBALL WITH ME?
I'M PRETTY GOOD.
SHU
YOU COME HERE A LOT?
FLICK
...
HE *WAS* SECRET POLICE AFTER ALL. HE WAS LISTENING TO US.
TMP TMP

YEAH. BUT MIMURA...
YOU LIED AGAIN.
IF NOTHING ELSE, TODAY...
...LOOKS LIKE A DATE TO OTHER PEOPLE, SO THAT'S WHAT IT IS.
OH!
THAT WAS NO LIE.
HUH...?
WHAT IS IT?
THE TRAIN...
WE'LL HAVE TO WAIT FOR THE NEXT ONE.
DON'T WORRY.
YEAH.
...THAT'S OKAY WITH ME.
ARE YOU STARTING TO FEEL...
...LIKE YOU'RE UNDER MY SPELL?
I'VE GOT THE ABSOLUTE NATIONAL DEFENSE SPHERE...
...OF THE A CUP.
WELL IN THAT CASE...
...YOU WANNA TAKE A WALK WITH ME UNTIL IT'S TIME TO GO?
THERE'S A RIVER NEARBY.

EPISODE II
Act 4...Burn
MY UNCLE...
...DIED LAST YEAR TOO.
?!
THEY SAY IT WAS AN ACCIDENT...
...BUT IT SEEMED A LITTLE FISHY TO ME.
FOR ONE THING, YOU SEE...
...HE WAS INVOLVED IN...
...ANTI-GOVERNMENT ACTIVITIES.

THIS RIVER'S FILTHY.

ANYWAY, THERE WAS THIS WOMAN IN MARUGAME...
...WHO'D BEEN CLOSE WITH MY UNCLE.
SHE'S BEEN DEAD A LONG TIME NOW, THOUGH.
ONE OF HER RELATIVES ...
...WAS GETTING HER THINGS IN ORDER...

...WHEN HE FOUND SOME OF MY UNCLE'S LETTERS.
HE CALLED ME UP...
... AND ...
...HE ASKED IF I WOULD COME AND GET THEM.
SO I WENT TO GET HIS LETTERS.
HMM ...
YOU SEE...
...I WAS ACTUALLY CLOSER TO MY UNCLE...
...THAN MY FATHER WAS.
AND MY UNCLE NEVER MARRIED...

WHAT IS IT?
OH, WELL... AH...
THERE IT IS!
IT'S OVER THERE.
?
I NOTICED IT BEFORE.
LET'S USE THIS LITTLE GUY.
IT'LL BE PERFECT FOR THE FIRE.
CLACK

A FIRE? ARE YOU BURNING SOME-THING?
WON'T WE GET IN TROUBLE DOING THAT IN THE MIDDLE OF THE CITY?
...
RUMMAGE
THIS WHOLE PREFECTURE IS PRACTICALLY RURAL.
RUSTLE
RUSTLE
IT'LL BE FINE.
RUSTLE
RUSTLE
RUSTLE
THOSE ARE...
SHUKO SHIMAMOTO
NOBUTAKA MIMURA
THEY'RE LETTERS...
...THAT MY UNCLE WROTE TO HER.

YOU'RE GOING TO *BURN* THEM?
WHY? DO THEY ALL HAVE SOMETHING DANGEROUS WRITTEN IN THEM?
THEY'RE JUST LOVE LETTERS.
NAKABU-CHO
KAGAWA PREFECTURE
NO, IT'S NOT LIKE THAT.
EVEN IF HE *HAD* BEEN INVOLVED IN ANYTHING ACTUALLY DANGEROUS...
SWIP
...THEY'RE ALWAYS OPENING MAIL...
...SO ANYTHING OF THAT NATURE WOULD'VE BEEN USED AS EVIDENCE AGAINST HIM.
THE LETTERS WERE IMPORTANT TO *THEM*.
BUT THEY'RE BOTH GONE NOW.
IT'S LIKE HOW SOMETIMES PEOPLE FIND THE LOVE LETTERS OF SOME OLD COMPOSER OR SOME-THING.
BUT THEY WERE MEANT TO BE PRIVATE. IT'S HUMILIAT-ING.
BUT...
...
I GUESS... MAYBE YOU'RE RIGHT...
...BUT STILL...
...EVEN LOVE LETTERS ARE IMPORTANT.

WELL...
WHETHER IT'S HUMILIATING OR NOT IS BESIDE THE POINT.
CHK
MY POINT IS...
...WHAT THEY FELT, WHAT THEY WROTE ABOUT...
...BELONGS TO THEM AND NO ONE ELSE.
WHOOSH
...
ESPECIALLY NOT TO THOSE COPS DOING THE GOVERNMENT'S WORK.
I DON'T WANT THEM GETTING THEIR *FILTH* ALL OVER THESE.
...THAT'S WHY...
...YOU SAID WE NEEDED TO GET OFF THE TRAIN.
YEAH.
...
ANYWAY, THERE SURE ARE A LOT.
THEY MUST HAVE REALLY LOVED EACH OTHER.
NO...

APPARENTLY...
...SHE WAS SEEING SOMEONE.
CRACKLE
IT WAS A ONE-SIDED LOVE ON MY UNCLE'S PART.
HUH?
OH...
THIS IS JUST A GUESS, BUT...
I THINK THE GUY SHE WAS WITH...
...WAS DEEP INTO ANTI-GOVERNMENT ACTIVITIES.
REALLY?
REALLY.
AND HE WAS EXECUTED FOR IT.

SINCE SHE WAS DATING HIM...
...THEY OBVIOUSLY INVESTIGATED HER.
AND SHE HAD A MENTAL BREAKDOWN.
THOUGH I'M SURE THE SHOCK OF HER LOVER'S DEATH WAS A PART OF IT.
...

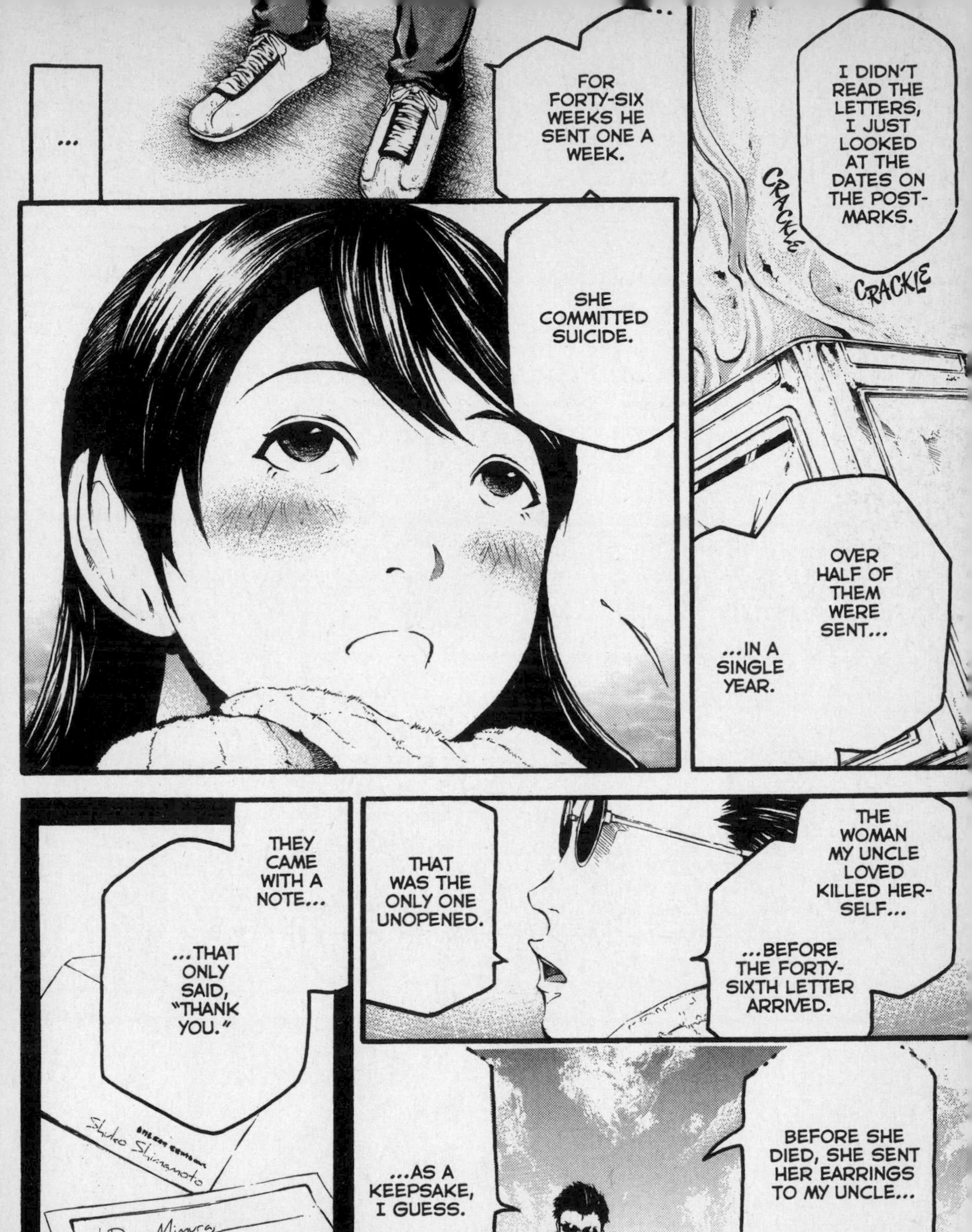
...
I DIDN'T READ THE LETTERS, I JUST LOOKED AT THE DATES ON THE POST-MARKS.
CRACKLE
CRACKLE
FOR FORTY-SIX WEEKS HE SENT ONE A WEEK.
...
OVER HALF OF THEM WERE SENT...
...IN A SINGLE YEAR.
SHE COMMITTED SUICIDE.

THE WOMAN MY UNCLE LOVED KILLED HER-SELF...
...BEFORE THE FORTY-SIXTH LETTER ARRIVED.
THAT WAS THE ONLY ONE UNOPENED.
BEFORE SHE DIED, SHE SENT HER EARRINGS TO MY UNCLE...
...AS A KEEPSAKE, I GUESS.
THEY CAME WITH A NOTE...
...THAT ONLY SAID, "THANK YOU."
Dear Mimura,
Thank you.

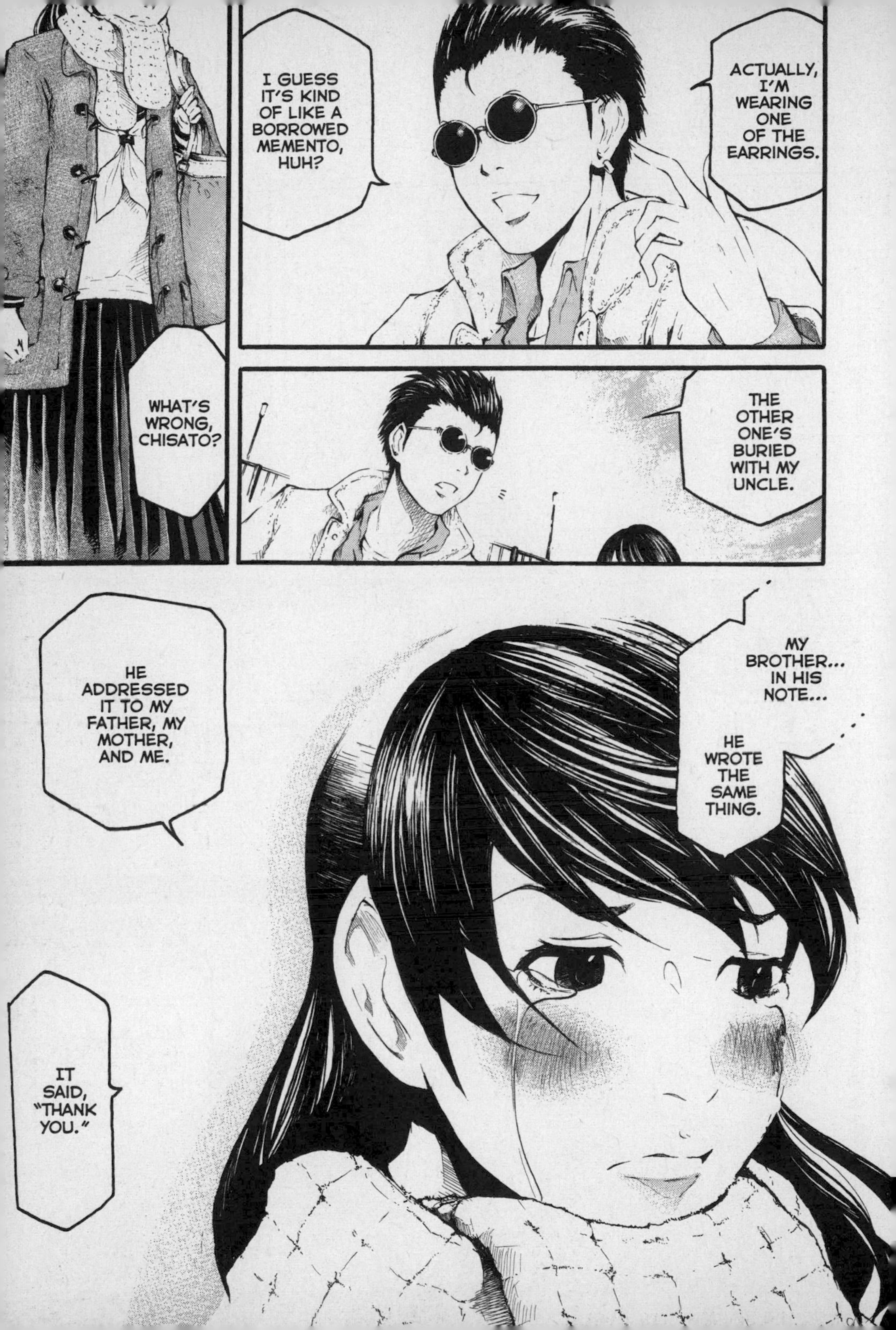
ACTUALLY, I'M WEARING ONE OF THE EARRINGS.
I GUESS IT'S KIND OF LIKE A BORROWED MEMENTO, HUH?
THE OTHER ONE'S BURIED WITH MY UNCLE.
WHAT'S WRONG, CHISATO?
MY BROTHER... IN HIS NOTE...
HE WROTE THE SAME THING.
HE ADDRESSED IT TO MY FATHER, MY MOTHER, AND ME.
IT SAID, "THANK YOU."

...OH.
BUT I...
CLUTCH
I WASN'T ABLE TO DO ANYTHING FOR MY BROTHER.
NOT LIKE WHAT YOUR UNCLE...
...DID FOR HER.
...
BUT AFTER MY BROTHER WAS DETAINED...
...I JUST TIPTOED AROUND HIM.
IT WAS BECAUSE OF HIM...
...THAT I BECAME INTERESTED IN OTHER COUNTRIES.
HE HAD LOTS OF FOREIGN BOOKS.
AND HE SHOWED ME...
...THAT THE WORLD IS A BIG PLACE.
...BUT I...
THAT'S NOT TRUE.

I'M SURE YOUR BROTHER WAS GLAD...
...JUST TO HAVE YOU THERE.
I'M A BIG BROTHER MYSELF.... SO I UNDERSTAND.
I DON'T KNOW ...
IT'S TRUE.
I DON'T CARE WHAT ANYONE SAYS TO ME...
...I JUST WISH HE WAS STILL ALIVE...
THAT'S...
...WHAT MY UNCLE SAID TOO.

MIMURA ...
WHY ARE YOU TELLING *ME* ALL THIS, WHEN IT MEANS SO MUCH TO YOU?
YOU TOLD ME ABOUT YOUR BROTHER, RIGHT?
IT'S ONLY FAIR.
BUT BEFORE THAT...
WHY DID YOU TELL ME ABOUT YOUR PRAYERS?
MAYBE I JUST THOUGHT I COULD SAY SOME-THING...
...*HMM*... WELL, THERE WAS SOMETHING ABOUT YOU TODAY.
YOU LOOKED LIKE A BALLOON ABOUT TO FLY AWAY.

...TO CATCH YOU.

I FELT THAT WAY WHEN I SAW YOU...
...ON THE PLATFORM AT RITSURIN STATION.
SOB SOB
CLUTCH
I'M JUST HOLDING YOU UP, THAT'S ALL. IT'S OKAY, RIGHT?
I'M NOT GOING TO MAKE A PASS AT YOU. I KEEP MY PROMISES.
... OKAY.

HEY.
IF I WERE YOUR BIG BROTHER... I WOULDN'T WANT YOU TO FLY AWAY.
OKAY.
THERE'S SOMETHING ELSE MY UNCLE SAID TO ME ONCE.
DON'T LET YOURSELF BE BLOWN ABOUT.
WHEN YOU FLY, LEAP FOR YOURSELF.
DO IT ON YOUR OWN TERMS, WHEN THE MOMENT IS RIGHT.
YEAH ...
GO TO ANOTHER COUNTRY SOMEDAY AND SEE IT WITH YOUR OWN EYES.
IF YOU DO THAT...
...I'M SURE YOUR BROTHER WILL BE HAPPY.
CRACKLE
CRACKLE
YEAH ...
YEAH ...

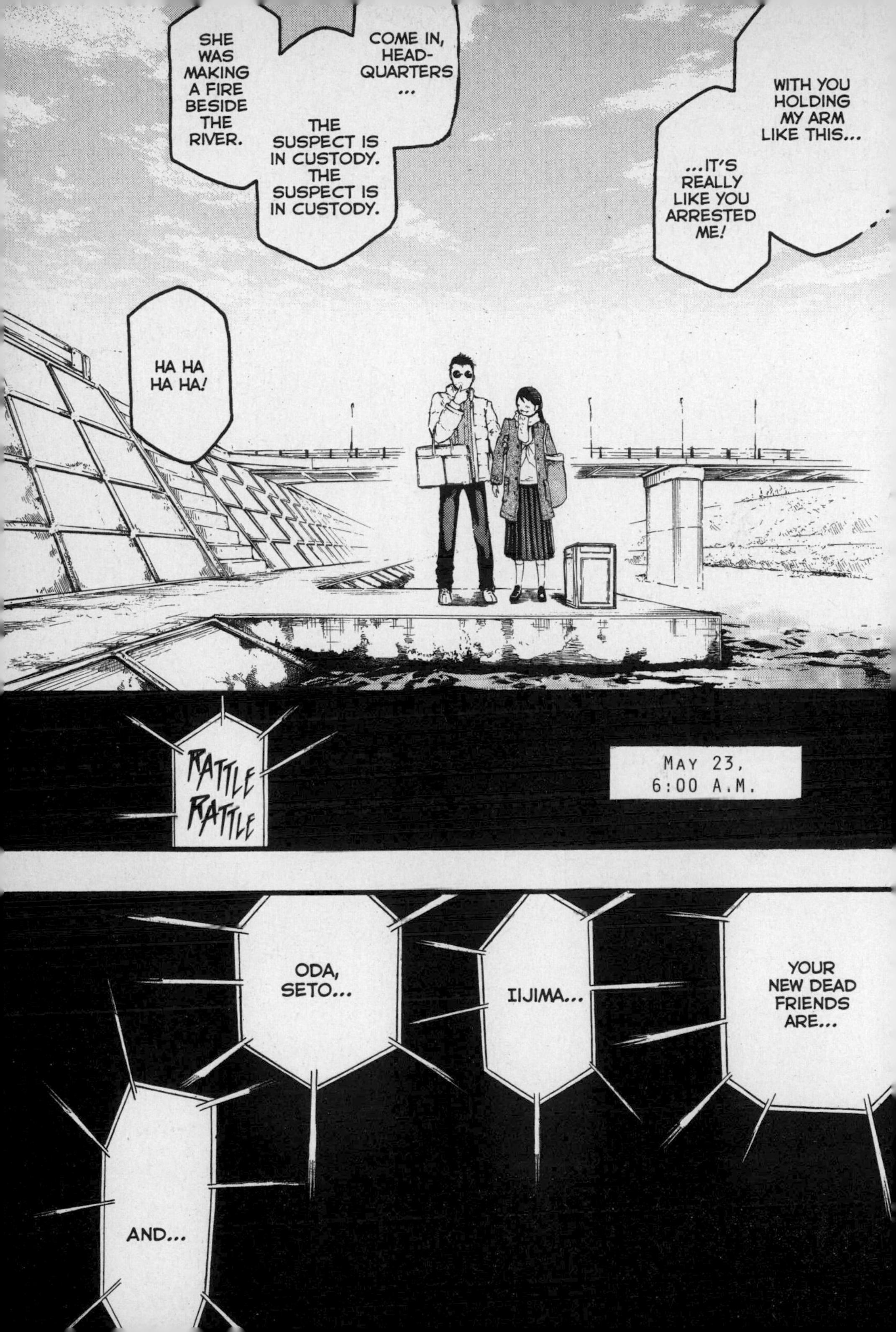
WITH YOU HOLDING MY ARM LIKE THIS...
...IT'S REALLY LIKE YOU ARRESTED ME!
COME IN, HEAD-QUARTERS...
THE SUSPECT IS IN CUSTODY. THE SUSPECT IS IN CUSTODY.
SHE WAS MAKING A FIRE BESIDE THE RIVER.
HA HA HA HA!
MAY 23, 6:00 A.M.
RATTLE RATTLE
YOUR NEW DEAD FRIENDS ARE...
IIJIMA...
ODA, SETO...
AND...

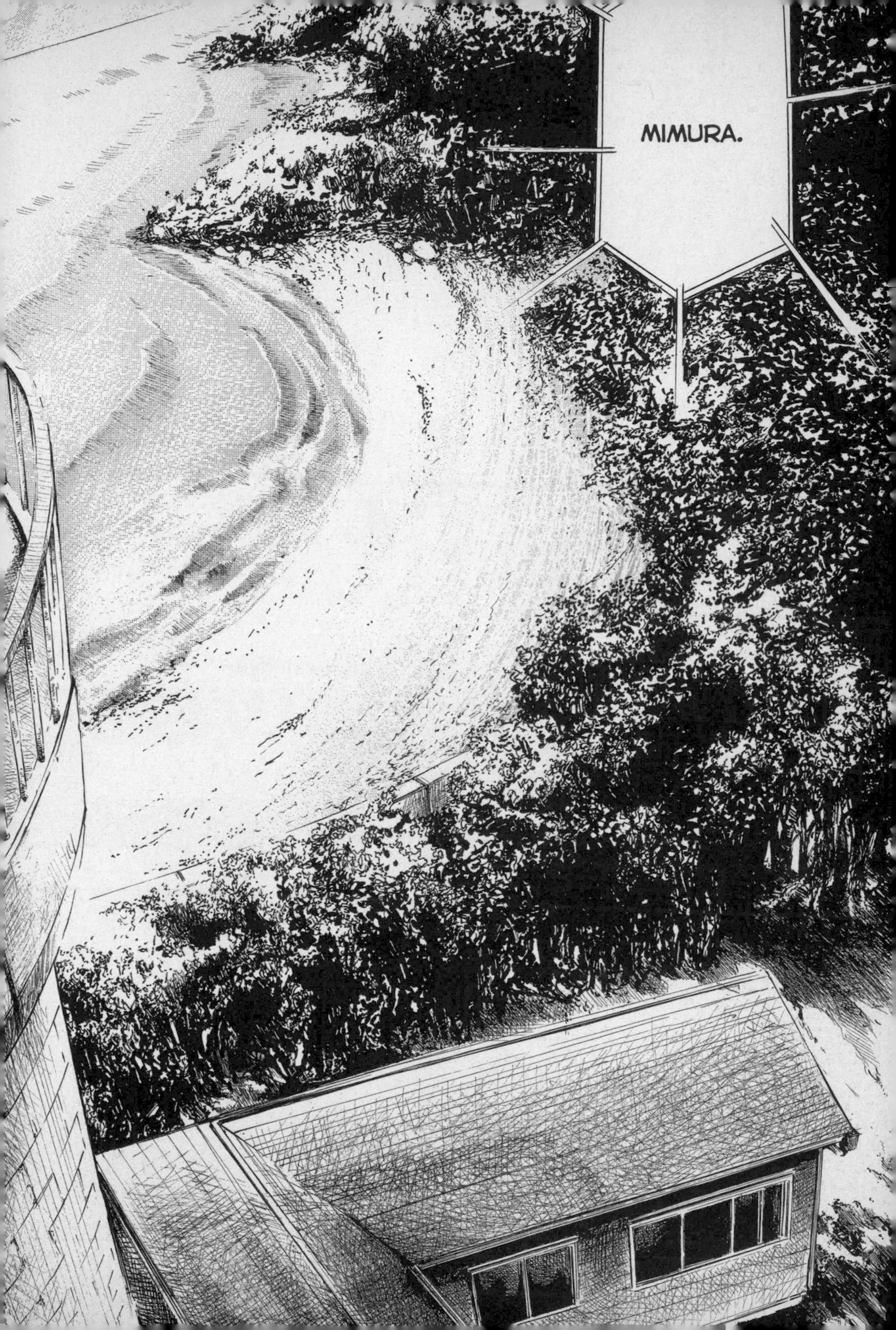
MIMURA.

RATTLE
GASP
THUD
CHISATO ...

Episode II
Act 5...Fly

HEY, MATSUI.

HERE...
...TAKE THIS.
FLAP

IT'S MY EMAIL ADDRESS... IF YOU'RE EVER IN SERIOUS NEED OF A HAND...
...YOU CAN REACH ME THERE.
...OKAY.

BUT IF IT LOOKS LIKE *TROUBLE*...
...BE SURE TO DITCH THAT NOTE.

... IF YOU COULD MEMORIZE IT, THAT WOULD BE THE BEST.
STARE

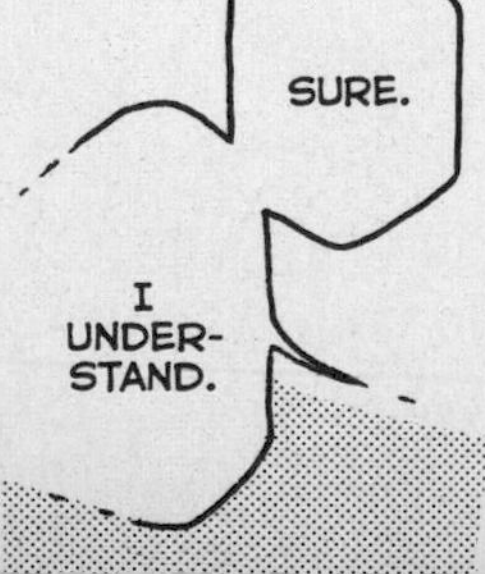
SURE.
I UNDER-STAND.

DONE.
YOU MEMORIZED THAT ALREADY? INCREDIBLE.
IF NOTHING ELSE...
...I HAVE A GOOD MEMORY.
ALL RIGHT.
SO...
...WE'RE FRIENDS NOW.
SHOVE
OH... YEAH.
BUT CONSIDERING WHAT HAPPENED WITH YOUR BROTHER ...
...AND MY UNCLE...
I THINK WE'RE BETTER OFF NOT TALKING AT SCHOOL.
YEAH ...
YOU'RE RIGHT.
SO... TODAY...
...WE'RE TAKING THE SAME TRAIN AND BUS...
...BUT THAT'S ONLY A COINCIDENCE.
AND BACK IN SHIROIWA, WE NEED TO ACT LIKE NOTHING HAPPENED. GOT IT?
BEEP

MATSUSHIMA SANCHOME STATION
...YEAH.
CHAK
I DON'T FEEL LIKE YOU'RE GOING TO FLY AWAY...
...NOT ANYMORE.
WHEN YOU FLY-
I'LL LEAP FOR MYSELF, WHEN THE MOMENT IS RIGHT.
YEAH.
ALL RIGHT.
THAT'S HOW IT IS.

And that's how it was.
After that...
...in school...
...Mimura and I didn't talk or anything.
But...
And then, oh, this is the worst part...
Sometimes, he...
what are you talking about?
...would give me a sign...
...that only I would understand.

MUNICIPAL GYMNASIUM
Today: Basketball Match with Kochi against
WHOOSH
SQUEAK
SQUEAK
MIMURA!
YOU'RE SO COOL!
...
HE'S SO POPULAR...
I'M GLAD I DON'T KNOW ANY OF THOSE GIRLS.
FIDGET

HE MADE ANOTHER THREE POINTER!
SWOOSH
SO COOL!
EEEEEEE!
SMIRK
WHA-
SHA
HE NOTICED ME!
HE SAW THROUGH MY DISGUISE...

I continued my lessons with the Wives Association...
...and that's how I happened to see something nice.
I was out on some errands for one of our events..
...when...

...Mimura...

...kept his promise.
(Of course, he might have been in the area...
...after coming to see that girl Hotta.)

WHO...
...DID IT?
MAY 23, 1:10 P.M.
WHICH ONE OF YOU TRIED...
...TO KILL US?
...CALM DOWN.
THIS IS ALL A MISUNDERSTANDING...
A MISUNDERSTANDING?

THIS IS NO MISUNDERSTANDING.
SOMEONE PRETENDING TO BE ONE OF US HAS SHOWN HER TRUE COLORS.
SURE, THAT'S RIGHT.
BUT MAYBE THAT SOMEONE IS YOU!
HARUKA!
DON'T!
...
...
!
Haruka?
What ...
...are you looking at?
!
SHE MUSTN'T!

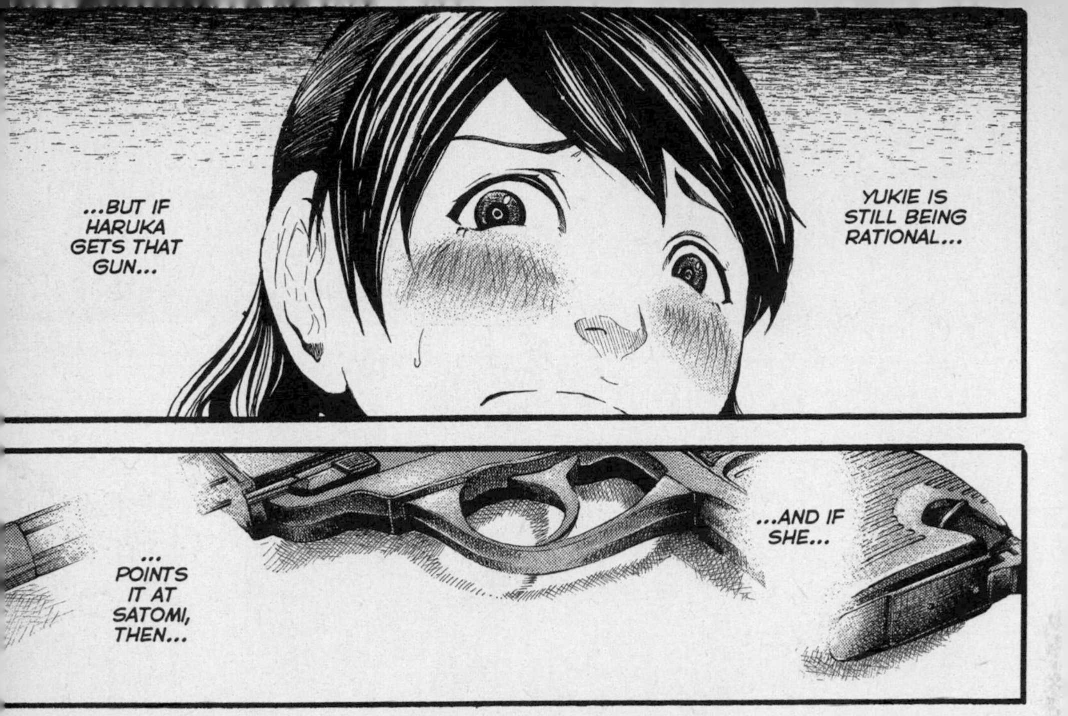
YUKIE IS STILL BEING RATIONAL...
...BUT IF HARUKA GETS THAT GUN...
...AND IF SHE...
... POINTS IT AT SATOMI, THEN...

NO. I HAVE TO DO SOMETHING...
THAT'S IT–IF I THROW IT OUT THE WINDOW...
SATOMI...
...MIGHT COME BACK TO HER SENSES.

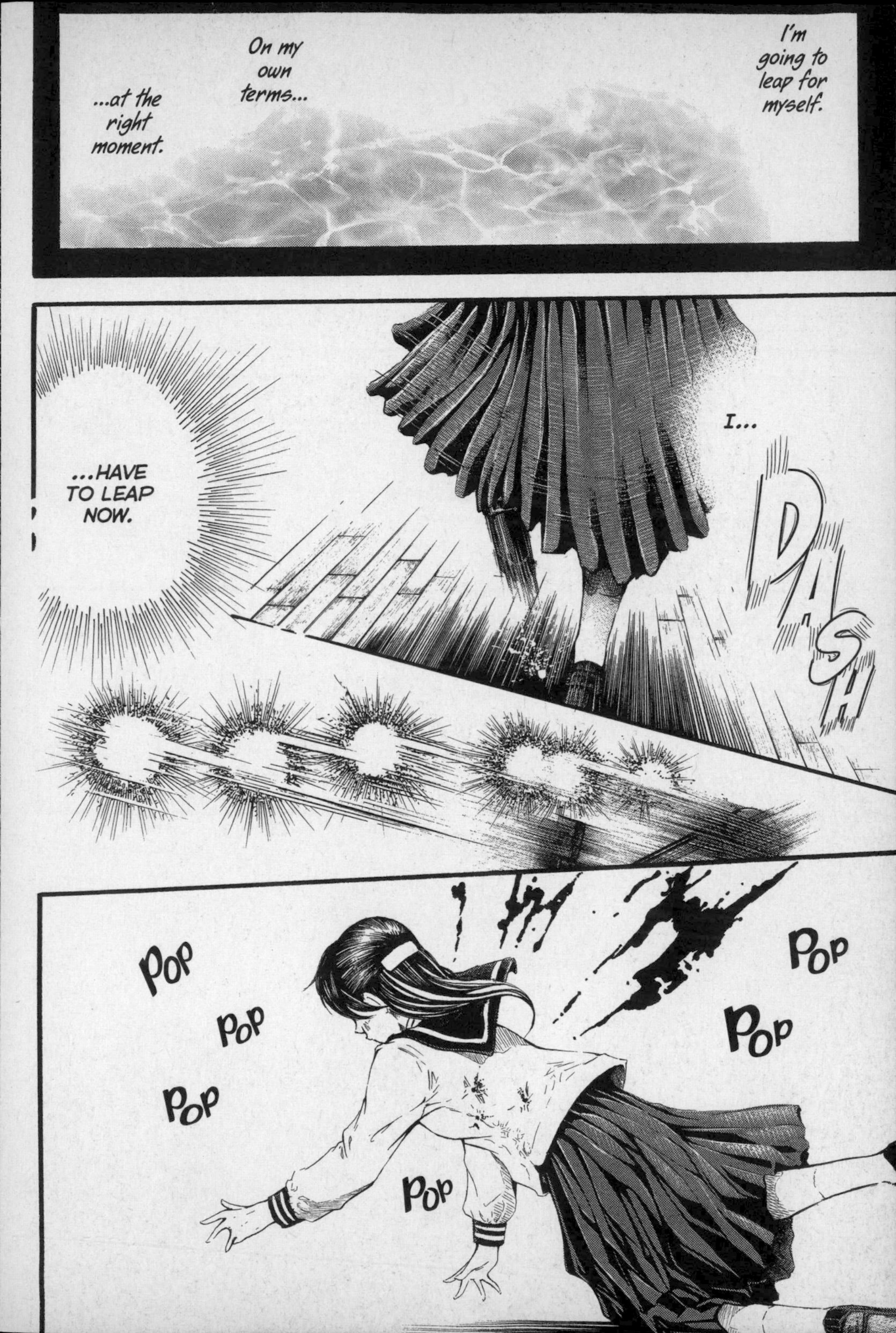
I'm going to leap for myself.
On my own terms...
...at the right moment.
I...
DASH
...HAVE TO LEAP NOW.
POP
POP
POP
POP
POP
POP

But...
Satomi thought I was going to...
...take the gun and shoot her.
How... stupid am I...?
Mimura...
I failed.

EVEN THOUGH I FINALLY LEAPED FOR MYSELF.
I'M SUCH A FOOL.

UM... EXCUSE ME.

?
YES?

I'M STUDYING PHOTOG-RAPHY AT THE...
...CREATIVE ARTS HIGH SCHOOL. MY NAME'S YOSHINO.
WE'RE DOING PORTRAITS RIGHT NOW...
...AND YOU TWO, UH... LOOK LIKE A NICE COUPLE.

I WAS WONDERING IF YOU'D MIND LETTING ME TAKE YOUR PICTURE.
...

ARE YOU...
...GOING TO DO AN EXHIBITION OR SOMETHING?
IF IT'S ONLY FOR PRACTICE...
...AND YOU WON'T SHOW IT OUTSIDE SCHOOL...
...EVEN IF IT TURNS OUT GOOD, THEN I DON'T MIND.
UNDERSTOOD. I PROMISE...
...I WON'T PUBLISH IT OUTSIDE SCHOOL.
ARE YOU SURE IT'S OKAY?
IT'LL BE FINE.
ON THE OFF CHANCE IT GETS OUT...
...WE JUST HAPPENED TO MEET HERE TODAY.
SHUP
WE JUST HAPPENED TO MEET, AND HAPPENED TO MODEL FOR A STUDENT.
IT'S ALL A COINCIDENCE.
OH, AND ACTUALLY...
...I HAVE ONE MORE FAVOR TO ASK.
WHAT'S THAT?

I'M DOING A THEME...
...WHERE I HAVE ALL MY SUBJECTS JUMP.
NOW...
YOU DON'T HAVE TO OVERDO IT OR ANYTHING, JUST BE JUMPING WHEN I PRESS THE SHUTTER. CAN YOU DO THAT?
I'M FINE WITH THAT.
THAT'S A 28MM LENS, RIGHT?
SO YOU'RE GONNA HAVE TO BACK UP TO TAKE IT, RIGHT?
HUH? WELL, BUT...
I PLAY SOME SPORTS...
I'LL DEFINITELY BE OUT OF FRAME.
...AND I'VE USED A FEW CAMERAS...
OH, OKAY. I SEE.
ALL RIGHT, WELL, UM...
WHAT DO YOU WANT TO DO FOR A SIGNAL?
I'LL COUNT IT DOWN. ONE, TWO, THREE, DAAH.
DAAH?
I'M *REALLY* GONNA JUMP, MATSUI. OKAY?
OKAY.
SO JUMP HIGH.
OKAY.

ONE.
CROUCH
TWO...
WHOA!
THREE!

Battle Royale
Angels' Border
EPISODE 2......END

BATTLE ROYALE
ANGELS' BORDER

END

Episode 1

Original Script

Major Characters

Yukie Utsumi ....Girl #2
Yuko Sakaki............Girl #9
Haruka Tanizawa...Girl #12
Yuka Nakagawa ... Girl #16
Satomi Noda........ Girl #17
Chisato Matsui...... Girl #19
Shuya Nanahara .. Boy #15

Written by Koushun Takami (with N-Cake)

SCENE 1

An island surrounded by the sea. There's some time before dawn. No lights are on across the island, including at the lighthouse. (The only exception is the school where the Nonaggressive Forces have set up a temporary post, though the building can't be seen from here.) The outlines of the mountains and the coast are faintly visible in the moonlight. The breaking waves are not that loud.

Haruka (Cap) First, there's something you need to know—I'm not normal.

Haruka (Cap) I haven't come out yet. (small inset of Sho Tsukioka [emphasize eyelashes and lips] saying, "What? No way! Really?")

Haruka (Cap) I didn't realize it until recently...

Atop the lighthouse, Yukie Utsumi is lying on her stomach, watching in all directions. She holds an Uzi submachine gun, and her face is smeared with soot as a form of nighttime camouflage. Around her neck is the distinctive device that was put around the necks of all the students. Several of her fingers appear to be bandaged; actually, it is volleyball athletic tape.

Haruka (Cap) And only because of her.

Haruka (quietly, peeking out from the doorway) "Yukie!" (Haruka also has the soot, and of course the collar, but her fingers are not taped.)

Yukie looks over her shoulder.

Haruka (holding out a cup on a tray) "How about some coffee?"

Yukie (smiling) "Sounds good. You made more?"

Haruka "You can't drink lying down like that. Let's trade."

Haruka takes the gun. As she does, the top button on Yukie's sailor-suit blouse comes undone, revealing much of her chest. For a split second, Haruka's eyes are caught by the beautiful contours of her skin from her neck down.

Haruka (Cap) Sometimes my breath catches—in awe that the one I love is so beautiful.

Haruka (blushing and looking away) (No, no! This is no time to think like that!)

Haruka "Yukie, your chest—you're exposing yourself." (You'd better put on camo there too.)

Yukie quickly puts her hands to her chest and does up her button. Haruka is lying on her stomach, keeping watch.

Yukie (still blushing, sipping the coffee) "Well, at a time like this, everyone's bound to let themselves go a bit."

Haruka	(keeping a watchful eye out, but smiling) "But really, you never have a hair out of place. You're our class leader, after all. And your father's so strict."
	Yukie's expression changes. Haruka looks like she realizes she said something wrong. Yukie looks away and presses her lips together.
Haruka (Cap)	And the one I love—she doesn't like it when people mention her father.
Haruka (Cap)	He's a soldier in the Nonaggressive Forces. Hardly anyone in class—or even the volleyball team—knows.
Haruka (Cap)	Soldiers aren't much loved in this country. One reason is a certain military research program.
Haruka (Cap)	And right now, we're in it.
Haruka (Cap)	I'm taking this watch very seriously—watching in case anyone comes to kill us. And if anyone comes to kill us...
Haruka (Cap)	I have to kill them.
	TITLE PAGE

SCENE 2

Haruka (Cap)	We were supposed to be going on a school trip. We were on the bus when they put us to sleep. It was around one in the morning when we awoke inside a school on an island we'd never seen....Over twenty-four hours have passed since then.
Haruka (Cap)	In that classroom, a strange man named Sakamochi told us we were about to begin the Program.
Sakamochi	"Today, you're all going to kill each other. How good for you! The last one alive gets to go back home!"
Haruka (Cap)	The Program is an annual military test conducted in our country, the Republic of Greater East Asia. The students of one chosen ninth-grade class kill each other over the sole survivor's chair.
Haruka (Cap)	I still don't understand what exactly they're testing, but I've known about it for as long as I can remember. Never had I imagined I'd be chosen. It's probably that way for everybody...like a car accident or a bad illness. Why me? But I'm trying not too think about it too much.
Haruka (Cap)	They showed us the corpse of our homeroom teacher, Mr. Hayashida, to prove this was no joke. He tried to protect us from being taken. And two of us were killed on the spot for disobeying orders. (Yoshitoki Kuninobu and Fumiyo Fujiyoshi)

SCENE 3

Atop the lighthouse.

Haruka (keeping watch, trying to lighten the mood) "So this...is a machine gun, huh. It's heavy, isn't it?"

Yukie (drinking her coffee) "Yeah."

Haruka "I still feel pretty ridiculous holding a thing like this."

Yukie "Yeah. But if I hadn't had mine..." (pulls out the Browning semi-automatic pistol from behind her back and looks at it) "We might not have been able to meet. I only felt like I could return to that school since I had this to see me through."

SCENE 4

Haruka (Cap) The forty of us (forty-two minus two) left one by one in our seating order. Disoriented, I ran into the night.

Haruka stands in what appears to be a village. Her back is to a wall as she looks around.

Haruka (Cap) But then I heard someone call my name.

Yukie "Haruka!"

Haruka (Cap) This might go without saying, but under these rules, every classmate is your enemy. But Yukie and I have been playing volleyball together—she the setter and me the hitter—ever since elementary school. We're best friends...and to me, now, she's even more.

Haruka (Cap) Anyway, I can trust her. Yukie would never try to kill me. And Yukie trusts me too, and that makes me feel truly happy.

The two girls tearfully embrace.

Haruka (Cap) Before we left the school, we were each given a weapon and some food. My weapon was a hammer (what was I supposed to do with that?), but Yukie had a pistol....

Yukie discovers a pistol in her daypack. A single piece of paper reads, "How to correctly handle a pistol."

Haruka (Cap) With that gun, Yukie was coming back.

Yukie We're going back to the schoolyard! Then we'll call out to everyone. We all need to come up with a plan together.

Haruka's expression is ambivalent.

SCENE 5

Atop the lighthouse.

Haruka	**Of course I'm scared. You heard what that man said in the class-room.**
Sakamochi	**The others are ready to kill.**
Haruka	**Everyones' faces.... It was so scary.**
Yukie	**Yeah.**
Haruka	**And yet...it's still hard to believe any of us would try to kill each other.**
Yukie	**(after a brief moment of thought) With what happened to Yumiko and Yukiko...**
Haruka (Cap)	**That was yesterday morning. From a mountaintop observation deck, the two girls called out through a megaphone for us to bring this all to a stop...only to be gunned down on the spot. We were able to see it from here.**

SCENE 6

Chisato Matsui comes running into the living space from the lighthouse tower.

Chisato	**That voice is coming from up in the mountains. It's Yumiko and Yukiko!**

The five girls emerge from the doorway atop the tower and look to the mountain. The sound of gunfire rings out, and their faces turn pale.

SCENE 7

Yukie	**You mean that might have been staged by the government?**
Haruka	**Yeah.**
Yukie	**But there was Akamatsu and Niida too.**

SCENE 8

Haruka (Cap)	Hiding in the thicket in front of the school, we saw two dead bodies. (Mayumi Tendo and Yoshio Akamatsu) From a distance, we couldn't see for sure, but Yuka Nakagawa, the first we called out to, said arrows were sticking out of their bodies.
Haruka (Cap)	And we'd just seen Kazushi Niida running away holding something like a bow.

SCENE 9

Yukie	Akamatsu was the first to go out, but he came back....Do you really think he did it for the same reason as us? If so, how can you explain Mayumi's death?
Haruka	Couldn't Akamatsu have suddenly run into Tendo? You know how easily scared he is...Maybe he just panicked and pulled the trigger.
Yukie	Either way, he still pulled the trigger. And then–whatever the reason–Niida must have killed Akamatsu.
Yukie	And... (goes quiet)
Haruka (Cap)	By that, did she mean Nanahara...?

SCENE 10

Haruka (Cap)	Partly due to what we'd seen, we decided to call out to only the girls. Skipping the boys, we had Yuka, Satomi Noda and Chisato Matsui...
Haruka (Cap)	Kaori Minami was next, but she ran when she saw us. I can't blame her. If you think about it, in thls game, someone being in a group isn't proof of her good intentions. She could turn on you at any moment. Or you could turn on each other....
Haruka (Cap)	Yoshimi Yahagi was the last one out, but we didn't call to her. She was in a group of delinquent girls. (three-shot of Mitsuko Souma, Hirono Shimizu, Yoshimi Yahagi) That was our only reason.

SCENE 11

Atop the lighthouse.

Haruka (Cap) In this game, every six hours, the names of those who died are announced.

Speakers all over the island; Sakamochi holding a microphone.

Haruka (Cap) Yoshimi Yahagi was announced soon after the game began, yesterday at noon.

Haruka This place is conspicuous. I keep thinking another person will come again.

Yukie At least we'll see them if they do.

Haruka Yeah, I guess...

Yukie ...It's like we're a nation.

Haruka A nation?

Yukie: Yeah. We've shut ourselves in here, choosing who we let in and who we exclude. Even before we came here, we'd already excluded Yahagi.

Haruka ...

SCENE 12

Haruka (Cap) After the five of us left the school, we wandered the island—we came across the couple Sakura Ogawa and Kazuhiko Yamamoto throwing themselves off the cliff.

Haruka (Cap) Once we arrived at this lighthouse and saw no one was inside, we decided to hole up here. A storage room was well-stocked with food and supplies. We barricaded the windows as quietly as we could... (Haruka using her hammer to board up a window)

Haruka (Cap) ...and we blocked the entrance. (the girls piling furniture)

Haruka (Cap) We decided the guard rotation first thing. We had no electricity or gas, but the water tank had a reserve, and we found some fuel tablets to cook with. As we kept up the rotation, sleeping in turn, the first night passed and another night came. As the time passed, the body count continued to rise.

Lighthouse living/dining room. Yukie and the girls are putting charcoal on their faces as camouflage. Haruka is helping Chisato. (Haruka says, "Camouflage?") They can hear the six p.m. announcement.

Sakamochi Um...Niida, Chigusa, Minami! Oh, I forgot. Tsukioka too. (Tsukioka:

	"What? No way!")
Haruka	(a bit shocked) Takako...and Kaori....
Haruka (Cap)	Not long after, two more of our classmates came here. They came, of course, only by chance...

SCENE 13

	Yuko Sakaki passing in front of the lighthouse.
Haruka (Cap)	First was Yuko Sakaki at around eight o'clock.
Haruka (Cap)	Yuko was half-delirious—we practically took her in under "protective custody." In class, she was timid and well-behaved, so none of us objected to allowing her into our "nation"—but if she'd had a gun, we might have thought twice about it.
Yukie	Where's your weapon? Is this it?
	Yuko is holding some kind of tactical police baton.
Yuko	Yes....just...this....
Haruka	(with a confused expression) ("Just this?")

SCENE 14

Haruka (Cap)	Then, about four hours later, I was keeping watch when I saw Shuya Nanahara. Just a little before, I'd heard a pitched gunfight in the distance.
	She hears snapping branches, and a body falls from the cliff overlooking the lighthouse and then is still. Haruka looks for his face through her binoculars, and though it is dark, she sees it is Shuya, and her face pales.
Haruka (Cap)	Nanahara was badly injured, but deciding whether or not to let him in caused a bit of turmoil. Yuko Sakaki, who we'd let join us not long before, firmly opposed it.
	Inside the lighthouse's living/dining room
Haruka	It's Nanahara. He's not moving at all! I'm going to take a look.
Satomi Noda	What are you talking about? Whoever did that might be close.
Yukie	(with barely noticeably conflicted expression, but speaking firmly) We'll wait two minutes. Then Haruka and I will go together. Somebody, go up top and give us cover.
	Yukie glances to Haruka. Haruka nods.

Yuko (suddenly shouting) No!!

The girls look to Yuko, who is wrapped up in a blanket on the couch.

Yuko He'll kill us all!

Haruka (Cap) Yuko told us she saw Nanahara kill Tatsumichi Oki. He split open Oki's head.

Haruka (Cap) Even if she had indeed seen what she thought she saw...I had a fairly good idea of who Nanahara was before, and I naturally assumed it must have been an accident. But Yuko wouldn't listen.

Haruka (Cap) In the end, we agreed to keep him locked in a room, and we brought him inside. But we couldn't even tell if he'd wake up again. Since I'm the strongest of us, I carried him in. (I'm even taller than he is.) He was still bleeding heavily, and his blood got all over me.

SCENE 15

Atop the lighthouse. Present time.

Haruka (sniffing her arm) I want to wash my clothes. I want to take a bath.

SCENE 16

Haruka (Cap) Anyway, we brought Nanahara inside and saw to his wounds.

A room in the lighthouse.

Yukie (pressing a cloth against Shuya's wound) Cover the windows so the light won't spill out. Chisato, bring me a needle and thread. I have a sewing kit in my bag. Yuka, do we still have hot water? If you have to boil more, make sure to hide the light!

In the living/dining room, Satomi is hugging Yuko, who is wrapped in her blanket.

Haruka (Cap) Nanahara is cheerful and kind. He's athletic, and good at the guitar. And he's good looking too. So it's only natural that he was popular with the girls. As I told you before, I'm not normal, so none of that matters to me....But now, in this particular situation, I had a reason to respect what Yukie wanted.

Haruka (Cap) Because I knew she was in love with him.

Haruka (Cap) And because I'm in love with her. Deeply.

SCENE 17

Atop the lighthouse.

Yukie	But you know, this still feels a little like a school trip to me.
Haruka	What? What do you mean?
Yukie	(grinning) I had this thought that maybe you're sick of me.
Haruka?	What?! Why? That's not true at all!
Yukie:	Yeah, I know. But...it's just like...you've been distant or something. Actually, it's felt that way for a little while now.

SCENE 18

Haruka (Cap)	To be honest, it's not like I didn't have an idea of what she meant. During a volleyball match, teammates share a kind of physical camaraderie. If you've ever seen a game on TV, you probably know what I'm talking about.
Haruka (Cap)	Girls in particular give each other hugs and the like.
Haruka (Cap)	But after I recognized what I felt toward Yukie, it became awkward for me.
Haruka (Cap)	To be blunt, I was clearly aware of my desire to feel her touch. Not that of a teammate in the middle of a game–this was a sexual desire.
Haruka (Cap)	Instead this made me feel like I mustn't let her touch me. I didn't want to dirty such a pure creature with my touch.

* * *

During a volleyball match, Yukie approaches Haruka for a hug, but Haruka seems evasive. Even during the high fives, Haruka looks away. Yukie's expression becomes confused.

SCENE 19

Atop the lighthouse, present. Haruka thinks back to how she hugged Yukie when they met each other the day before, just after the game began.

Haruka	(blushing) (Yesterday I lost myself and put my arms around her.) (But it wasn't like that.)

* * *

Haruka's memory of the day before. She embraces Yukie but quickly realizes what she's done and pushes herself away. Yukie says "What?" and appears confused.

* * *

Atop the lighthouse, present.

Yukie — **(peers into Haruka's face, looking a bit concerned) Haruka? I'm sorry, I must sound crazy.**

Haruka — **(snapping out of her memory) Oh, no, well...it-it's not quite like that. Look, didn't you tell me about that creep who felt you up on the train—in February, wasn't it? You called him out, but he acted innocent and then threatened you. You said you felt awful.**

SCENE 20

Haruka (Cap) — **She told me the story around the same time I noticed my feelings for her.**

On a nearly full train.

Yukie — **(over her shoulder) Stop it!**

Businessman — **What? She's lying! Give me a break here. (looking about) You all saw. I had both hands on my newspaper this whole time, didn't I?**

Some Old Lady — **Hmph. Kids these days think everything's about them.**

SCENE 21

In the corner of a room, a crying Yukie tells Haruka the story.

Yukie — **When he was getting off the train, he whispered to me...**

SCENE 22

Man — **(whispering) Speak out like that next time, and I'll kill you, you little shit.**

The door closes. Still inside the train, Yukie trembles.

SCENE 23

Atop the lighthouse.

Haruka (Cap)	Seeing her then made me all the more aware of my feelings.
Yukie	Yeah, I said that....But what of it?
Haruka	A-after that, I thought...you might not want anyone to touch you.
Yukie	(stunned, but smiling) What? That's completely different. He was some creepy man who I don't know, and you're a girl who's my friend.
Haruka	B-b-b-b-but girls can be creepy too, right?
Yukie	(a bit mystified) I suppose...But no, that's different. Men are stronger than women, yeah? Nothing's lower than someone who does something nasty just because their victim can't stop them.
Haruka	But there're burly women too, right? Like me. M-my grip strength is 84 pounds. A-and that's my right. My left is–
Yukie	You're not burly. Okay, you're taller than me, but so what? You're more feminine and delicate...You're a very pretty girl.
Haruka (Cap)	I'm not talking about my looks... And the compliments aren't helping.
Yukie	(confidently) You need to have confidence. (blows air out her nose)
Haruka	(completely flushed)
Haruka (Cap)	No...If I had confidence now, that'd only be trouble.
Yukie	(appearing mollified for now) I see. Well, if that's what it is...I understand. But from now on, you can touch me all the time.
Haruka	(blushing even more) T-touch you...
Yukie	Well, who knows how much longer we'll have, anyway.

Both girls instantly become sober.

SCENE 24

Haruka (Cap)	This game has a time limit. It goes on until only one of us is alive. But if 24 hours pass without a single death...

Collar

Haruka (Cap)	...these devices clamped around our necks will explode.
Haruka (Cap)	There's more–this island is partitioned into a grid. Each announcement adds to a list of sectors we have to avoid... Failing to do so will also trigger the explosives. As time passes, we have less and less of the island open to us.

Map

Haruka (Cap)	We don't know when this lighthouse will be designated forbidden. And even if that hasn't happened by the time everyone else is dead and only the seven of us here remain...
Haruka (Cap)	Unless we kill each other, we'll only have 24 hours left.
Haruka (Cap)	In other words, we have no hope. We either die together as seven, or we draw a lottery for six of us to kill ourselves so that one can live.
Haruka (Cap)	If it comes to that...I'd want Yukie to survive. (Sorry, everyone else.)
Haruka (Cap)	But I know Yukie wouldn't be able to bear Nanahara's death.
Haruka (Cap)	Just as I wouldn't be able to bear hers.

SCENE 25

Yukie	Anyway, well, I didn't know you were being so considerate of me. Actually, I was starting to think that I was the one acting funny—always trying to be so clingy. I figured that if you maybe wanted to be around the other girls more than me...that might make me feel a little lonely, but there was nothing I could do about it. But...
Yukie	When I first saw you yesterday, I was so relieved. I could count on you. If not for you, I don't think I would've been able to seek out the others.
Yukie	(facing Haruka) You're my best friend, Haruka... And isn't it just like a school trip to figure that out?
Haruka (Cap)	Friend, huh.... What else did I expect... (I guess that means "lover" is out of the question.) (And how long is she going to go on?)
Haruka	(setting those feelings aside) You really are incredible, Yukie.
Yukie	Me?
Haruka	You've got such composure. Out here, most people couldn't think like that.
Yukie	Really? I wonder.
Haruka	Really.
Haruka (Cap)	And that part of Yukie is just one of the reasons I love her.

SCENE 26

The coffee left in the cup is no longer giving off steam.

Yukie	What's everyone up to?
Haruka	Umm...Chisato is keeping watch below, and everyone else is asleep.

	Well...I don't think Yuko is sleeping. I think Satomi is awake too. (Yuka is totally out.)
Yukie	Were you able to sleep?
Haruka	Yeah, I was. When I woke up, Chisato asked if I wanted coffee, and I thought I'd bring you some. It's not very warm, but it's still drinkable, right?
Yukie	(giving a thumbs-up and taking another drink) Yeah. Either way, it's gone cold now, but it tastes good.
Haruka (Cap)	We posted someone on watch below to look out over the seaward side, which isn't visible from atop the tower. All electricity and phone lines have been shut off, but we found some batteries and a radio, and the person on guard below listens for the regularly scheduled DHK news reports. Who knows, even the weather forecast might prove useful out here.
Haruka	It's a little heartbreaking to listen to that radio.
Haruka	All the broadcasts are the same as always. It makes you ask what we're all doing out here.
	In the living space below, Chisato Matsui watches out a window with headphones on. We can't hear the radio, but it might be playing music. Chisato suddenly begins to cry.
Haruka	I checked in on Nanahara, but he still wasn't moving at all.
Yukie	(visibly worried) I see...
Haruka	He'll be fine. I carried him yesterday, and I could hear his heartbeat... I can't really explain it, but I knew that he'd be all right.
Yukie	(a little more cheerful) Yeah...
Haruka	(looking away from Yukie) Hey, Yukie, when he wakes up, you should tell him how you feel.
Yukie	Huh?
Haruka	Oh, come on. You don't need to hide it from me. (Didn't you just say I'm your best friend?)
Haruka (Cap)	Well, I am hiding something from her.
Haruka (Cap)	And probably forever.
	Yukie lies down beside Haruka. Yukie takes out the Browning. Haruka looks a little puzzled, but continues.
Haruka	Your speech yesterday was incredible...It was because of how truly you want to save him, right?
Yukie	My speech...
Haruka	You know, "Let's share our hope," was it?
Haruka (Cap)	Actually, Yuko wasn't the only one uneasy about bringing Nanahara in. But then Yukie said...

Yukie — We're here together because we share hope. If we refuse to help an injured person right in front of our eyes, that hope will become nothing but a fraud. Am I wrong?

* * *

Yukie — Oh, that...

Haruka — (nods)

Yukie — (dropping her eyes) No...I'd like to say it was just common sense... but it was my personal feelings. Otherwise, there'd be no point in us taking up our guns and turning them to the outside.

Haruka — ...

Yukie — I said we were like a nation, right?

Haruka — ...Yeah.

Yukie — Not that long ago, my father and I talked about this experiment.

Haruka — (quite surprised) Really?

Yukie — Yeah.

Haruka — Did he tell you anything that would help?

Yukie — No, of course not. He's assigned to a desk job, totally out of his field, and even supposing he does know anything, he surely has to keep it secret—even from his family.

Haruka — Oh...Yeah, I suppose so. But what did he say, then?

Yukie — It was when I went into ninth grade. I knew there was a chance we'd be chosen, right? It's so rare of a chance that I think we all mostly try not to think about it... But even with that small chance, I wanted to ask him about it—especially since his division is in charge of running the Program.

Haruka — What did you ask him?

Yukie — I asked him, "What's the experiment? Why do we make junior high students kill each other?"

Haruka — ...Did he tell you?

Yukie — No. He said he didn't know. But he did offer a guess.

Haruka — A guess? What was it?

Yukie — "Shared fear."

Haruka — Fear?

Yukie — He said that enemies are good for bringing a country together, but so can hardship when shared equally by all. He thought that might have been the reason they came up with the experiment. All the many children who die every year are a shared sacrifice, uniting the nation. And we do have enemies, so that's why junior high kids have to die in these experiments. Right now, it's us.

Haruka	(her expression changes) ...That's stupid!
Yukie	(nodding) Yes, it's stupid. That's what I said to my father. And I said that if that's what our country's like, I don't want it. But he told me that he also thinks this experiment itself is stupid, but that the preservation of the nation is necessary.
Haruka	...
Yukie	That was the extent of our talk. But a little while later, he bought me a cell.
Haruka	A cell? Like a cell phone?
Yukie	Yeah. He said that if anything happened, I should call him immediately, and he'd do what he could to help. But...
Haruka	But?
Yukie	I refused to take it. I said it was ridiculous, and that if his beloved country asks for his daughter, he should just go right ahead and give her to it. I said that if he wants me to die I'll be glad to do it.
	A cell phone broken, smashed on the floor.
Haruka	...
Haruka (Cap)	Yukie is always so calm and well-mannered.... Did she really talk like that to her father?
Yukie	Of course, even if I had that phone now, I don't believe it would change anything. None of the phones get reception out here anyway. But ever since that happened, things between us were strained. I never really talked to him....
	Yukie stops speaking. Haruka looks and sees she is crying.
Yukie	Why did I say such a thing to him? He was just looking after me the best he could. Now I'll never see him again... Why did I say such a thing?
Haruka	...
Yukie	I want to tell him I'm sorry. How must he have felt, having his only daughter say that to him?
	Yukie keeps crying. The teardrops fall onto the Browning in her hands.
Haruka (Cap)	Dear God, the person I love is incredibly kind. She cares about her family.
	Nighttime island scenery.
Haruka (Cap)	And that person is crying.
	Haruka's expression is resolute, yet calm.
Haruka (Cap)	This I swear: what I'm about to do, I'm not doing out of lust.
	Haruka reaches out.
Haruka (Cap)	I just want to give her encouragement. She's very important to me...

Haruka puts her arm around Yukie's shoulder. Yukie looks up at her.

Haruka (Cap) ...And I love her. (Tsukioka's voice: "Hey, isn't that a bit lustful after all?")

Haruka Yukie, let's make it to the nationals this year.

Yukie The nationals? You mean the tournament? Like volleyball?

Haruka (Cap) Oh, why is this little thing all I can find to say?

Haruka (nodding) Of course! We'll go with the whole team. You can't give up now. We might still have some chance. Something might happen to cancel all this...or maybe Nanahara has an idea. Anyway, the very moment you give up, you lose. It's just like a volleyball match. Our opponents have taken every point and every set. It's match point, and we haven't scored once. But we can't think like we've already lost. We mustn't.

Yukie ...

Haruka (Cap) ...But it's the best I can do.

Haruka "Let's share our hope."

Yukie (smiling, wiping her tears) ...That's right.

Haruka You can apologize to your father when we get off this island. That's how you have to think.

Yukie Yeah... You're right.

Yukie reaches out and hugs Haruka. Haruka freezes for a moment, but then they look at each other and smile.

Yukie Thank you, Haruka.

Haruka (embarrassed, looking away again) (but keeping her arms around Yukie) I hope Nanahara wakes up soon.

Yukie Me too.

Haruka Nanahara will wake up this afternoon. I can feel it.

Yukie What? You can?

End

Additional Pattern 1

Chisato Matsui runs to pick up the gun and is shot by Satomi Noda.

Yukie Utsumi reaches for her gun and is also shot.

Haruka Tanizawa tries to pick up Yukie's gun and is also shot.

Yuka Nakagawa lies on the floor, her face swollen from the poison.

Only Satomi and and Yuko Sakaki remain.

Satomi You... You're different, right?

But Haruka sits up and shoots Satomi in the head with Yukie's gun.

Satomi's machine gun rips through Haruka once more, and Haruka is blown backward.

Then Satomi too falls.

Yuko stands frozen in the room.

Additional Pattern 2

Chisato Matsui runs to pick up the gun and is shot by Satomi Noda.

Yukie Utsumi reaches for her gun and is also shot.

Haruka Tanizawa tries to pick up Yukie's gun and is also shot.

Yuka Nakagawa lies on the floor, her face swollen from the poison.

Only Satomi and and Yuko Sakaki remain.

Satomi **You... You're different, right?**

But Haruka sits up and shoots Satomi in the head with Yukie's gun.

Haruka (Cap) **Why does wanting only to protect someone end up with having to hurt someone else?**

Satomi's machine gun rips through Haruka once more, and Haruka is blown backward.

Then Satomi too falls.

Yuko stands frozen in the room.

Haruka (Cap) **All I wanted was to protect her...to protect the one I love.**

Reprise of Yukie and Haruka smiling.

Episode 2
Original Script

Major Characters

Chisato Matsui...... Girl #19
Shinji Mimura .... Boy #19

* * *

Yukie Utsumi ....Girl #2
Yuko Sakaki............Girl #9
Haruka Tanizawa...Girl #12
Yuka Nakagawa ... Girl #16
Satomi Noda........ Girl #17

Act 1	Encounter
	Some time near November. Early on this Saturday afternoon, the midtown train station (Ritsurin Station) of the elevated JR tracks is nearly empty. Chisato Matsui waits on the train platform. Though this is a day off, she is wearing her school uniform (with the jacket), and is carrying a large tote bag. She is leaning against a support column and lets out a troubled sigh. A train pulls in.
	She gets onto the train and looks for a seat.
Chisato	(Umm...)
	Chisato sees an open spot next to the aisle in one of the forward-facing seats, but the man next to it is wearing overtly suspicious sunglasses (like Shunsaku Kudo's glasses from the TV series *Detective Story*).
Chisato	(Yikes.) (nervous sweat drop)
	Chisato looks for another seat. A little farther away, on the opposite side, a young salaryman occupies two seats while fiddling with his cell phone. He's certainly noticed Chisato but pretends not to have.
Chisato	(Darn. Guess I'll stand...)
Voice from behind	—tsui! Matsui!
	Chisato notices and looks back over her shoulder. The man in the sunglasses is calling to her.
Chisato	(with a suspicious expression) (Who's that?)
	The man lifts up his sunglasses. It's her classmate Shinji Mimura.
Chisato	Mi-Mimura?
Mimura	(grinning, gesturing to the open seat next to him) This one's open. Take a seat.
	Still a little hesitant, Chisato does as he suggests.
Mimura	(pocketing his sunglasses) Want me to put your bag up on the rack?
Chisato	No, it's not that heavy. (hugging the bag on her lap)
Chisato (Cap)	In my class, Shiroiwa Junior High Eighth Grade Class B, there are 41 students—21 girls and 20 boys. Compared to the other boys, Mimura has more of a certain kind of history.
Chisato (Cap)	Though only in eighth grade, he's a star on the basketball team, and he's way more knowledgeable than our teachers. And his looks are...well, as you can see, pretty cool. So maybe it's only natural...
Chisato (Cap)	...that everyone says he's a playboy. Even though he's only in eighth grade, the other kids debate whether or not he carries a...c-c-c-con-con...One of those...rubber things. (pictures a condom and goes faint)

Mimura | What's with the uniform? This isn't a school day.

Chisato | Oh, no reason.

Chisato (Cap) | At school, we've hardly ever talked, and yet he's smiling at me like this. If I hadn't heard what the other girls in Class B said about him, even I might get taken in by it and smile too.

The local train hasn't left the station yet. An elderly woman with a cane steps onto the train. She walks near the man occupying two seats by himself, but he shows absolutely no sign of letting her sit. Chisato hurriedly takes hold of her bag to stand up, but Mimura stands first and calls out to the woman.

Mimura | Ma'am! Take my seat.

The woman turns around and gives Mimura a tiny bow. Mimura helps her to his seat, then grasps one of the hanging straps. The train begins to move.

Woman | Thank you. That's very nice of you.

Mimura | Oh, it's nothing.

Chisato looks again at the man in the two seats, but he remains entirely indifferent.

Chisato | (What a creep. Wh–)

Mimura bends down and blocks her sightline.

Mimura | Don't look. Let him be. Meddle with stupid and you'll catch it.

Chisato | ...

Mimura | Someone once wrote that evil is just a matter of stupidity. That's true on many levels, but in this case... Huh?

Mimura's sentence is cut off when someone suddenly pulls at the back of his coat collar. Mimura turns to find that man there.

Man | By "stupid," did you mean me?

Mimura | (looking over his shoulder with a grin) Oh? So you heard?

The man grabs the chest of Mimura's coat. He's a bit taller than Mimura.

Man | I was working all night, and I'm tired. I'm better than some old woman looking so nice off of her pension check. And you, you're a student, right? Don't give me that look like you're better than me when you're living off your parents' money!

Mimura listens with a smile on his face until something suddenly catches his eye and his expression changes.

Mimura | (dropping his attitude and lowering his eyes) I'm sorry. I didn't mean it.

Man | What do you mean you didn't mean it?! You think I'm not serious? I'll fucking kill you! You better watch yourself.

The man lets go of Mimura and returns to his seat. Inside the carriage, the atmosphere is tense.

Announcement — **The next stop is Kitacho. Kitacho.**

Mimura leans in to Chisato and whispers.

Mimura — **Sorry to ask you this, but would you get off with me at the next stop?**

Chisato — **What?**

Mimura — **There's a reason. Please trust me.**

Chisato — **(blushing a little at Mimura's serious expression) Oh...okay. (If I stay on the train, it'll be awkward now anyway. I can just wait out there for the next train.)**

The train pulls into a station lined with an assortment of small shops, storehouses and residences. It's an unmanned station, and no riders are waiting on the platform. (The exit is to the left.)

Mimura — **Okay, let's get off.**

The two get off the train. The man is still fiddling with his cell phone looking irritated. The other riders appear vaguely uncomfortable, but the old woman bows to Chisato and Mimura again.

No one else exits the train at this stop.

Mimura — **All right. Let's escape.**

Chisato — **Escape?**

Mimura immediately begins walking. Having not been given a choice, Chisato follows him. They leave the station and take a small street.

Mimura — **(as they walk) You know about the Youth Corps, right?**

Chisato — **Uh...yeah.**

Chisato (Cap) — **In our country, the Republic of Greater East Asia, many organizations on many levels–in each region, in schools, and in workplaces, and so on–do many different of activities in many different of settings in order to bring about the nation's ideals... At least, that's the story.**

Mimura — **This month, they're doing an "improve public manners" drive. I saw the conductor reporting what happened. Likely somewhere around the next stop or so, a crowd of the Youth Corps will rush onto the train, and they'll give that guy a talking to. There might even be police with them, and he might be detained.**

Chisato — **The conductor reported it? How could you tell?**

Mimura — **I saw him on the radio, so I'm sure of it.**

Chisato — **So...why do we have to escape?**

The two emerge onto a wide, busy street.

Mimura — **(flagging a taxi) Well, it takes two sides to quarrel, so they might decide to question us. And if we wait for the next train, they might come find us. I don't want that. Today, there's certain...factors that make the police mean trouble for me. If I leave you behind, my identity will end up being revealed. I'm sorry, but please come with me**

for a little while.

Chisato ("Factors?")

Mimura We'll transfer to the Kotohira Line and take a bus back to Shiroiwa. That won't be a problem, right?

A taxi pulls up in front of them. But Chisato clutches her bag and hesitates.

Mimura (grinning) What's wrong? You don't trust me? Because of my reputation? Don't worry, I never hit on girls that don't have at least a 38-inch bust.

Chisato (pulling her bag into her chest) Urk.

Mimura (suddenly serious) I promise. I won't do anything funny. I won't think anything funny.

Chisato sighs.

Chisato I don't get the kind of allowance to be able to pay for a taxi.

Mimura I'll pay, of course. And the bus and the train fare too. Don't worry about a thing!

Act 1 The Battle

Chisato Matsui's number comes up and she leaves the school. She gasps when she sees the bodies of Yoshio Akamatsu and Mayumi Tendo. She hears a soft, yet sharp whisper. "Chisato!" She looks toward the thicket ahead. She can't see very clearly, but she sees what appear to be several girls hiding in the bushes. One of them (Yukie), standing half out of the bushes, is holding a gun. Another behind her (Satomi) has a machine gun.

Girl (Yukie Utsumi) (waving her arms) Chisato! Hurry!

Chisato Yukie!

Inside the thicket, Chisato and Yukie embrace.

Chisato Yukie! Everyone!

Satomi Shhh. Don't shout. The next one'll come soon.

Chisato Oh, sorry. But the next is....

Chisato looks around. In addition to Yukie and Satomi, only Haruka Tanizawa and Yuka Nakagawa are present.

Chisato Is this all of you?

Haruka Yeah.

Chisato (hesitantly) Oh...Did...Mimura come out just before me?

Haruka Mimura already went off somewhere. (Why...?)

Chisato But...he....

She thinks back to before she left the classroom. As Mimura leaves just ahead of her, he holds up his right hand, stands up his thumb, pointer, and middle fingers, and gives her a small wave. Noticing the gesture, Chisato clutches her left hand to her chest. The only students left in the room are those yet to depart—Kyoichi Motobuchi (Boy #20), Kaori Minami (Girl #20), Kazuhiko Yamamoto (Boy #21), and Yoshimi Yahagi (Girl #21). The corpses of Yoshitoki Kuninobu and Fumiyo Fujiyoshi are on the floor. Sakamochi stands on the teacher's podium, flanked by soldiers carrying rifles.

* * *

Chisato seems unable to accept Mimura's departure.

Act 1 End

Act 2 Part

Inside the taxi.

Mimura **Umm... Take us to the Matsushima Sanchome Kotohira Line Station, please.**

The driver nods and the taxi takes off.

Mimura **Oh, I think if you turn up there, it'll be faster. That road will take us straight to the highway.**

Driver **Yeah, it does... You sure know a lot, mister.**

The driver glances at Mimura in the rearview mirror.

Driver **...Are you a police detective? Does that make the girl your prisoner?**

Mimura **What? No, if I was a detective, I wouldn't be catching a train. I'd have you take us the rest of the way to the prefectural HQ.**

Driver **That's right. But still...you have that look about you.**

They soon arrive at Matsushima Sanchome Station, and the two exit the taxi. They are near the center of the city and alongside a highway, so many cars are passing by. (Matsushima Sanchome is a fictional station. When you are drawing the sign, the next station up is "Matsushima Nichome" and the next station down is "Okimatsushima," both of which exist.)

Driver **Thank you.**

Mimura **(Watching the taxi drive off, grinning dryly) He called me a detective. Do I look that old?**

Chisato **...Do you think it's those sunglasses?**

Mimura **Maybe. But calling you a prisoner was pretty harsh.**

Chisato **(thinks for a moment, then:) Maybe it's because I seem gloomy.**

Mimura | Really? I don't think that's true at all. You're really cute, Matsui.

Chisato gives a little start. Mimura is grinning.

Chisato | (So that's how he does it, with a casual compliment like that...) (Watch out, watch out.)

Chisato | (regains her composure) So we'll get off at Shido, then take a bus?

Mimura | Right. Let's look at the train schedule.

The two walk together.

Chisato | (Actually... I did meet with a detective because of my brother....)

Chisato sighs again. Mimura notices, but goes on ahead to read the schedule posted inside the station. Here and there inside the station are a mix of the elderly and students likely on their way home from school club activities. In the background, a male student with a camera (Yoshino, who will appear in Act 5) is talking with an older man.

Mimura | Hmmm... Looks like we just missed it. The next one's in twenty minutes.

Chisato | (pointing at a bench alongside the wall) You want to sit?

Mimura | No, let's duck into the restaurant over there. I've put you through all this trouble, so I'll buy you something.

Mimura starts walking and Chisato follows.

Chisato | You don't have to. I can pay for tea, at least.

Mimura | You don't have to worry about paying. Have you heard of computer shareware?

Chisato | Actually, yes. Those are the programs people put on the net, and then other people give them money.

Mimura | Yeah. I've taken in some money doing that. So don't worry about it.

Chisato | (honestly impressed) That's amazing! You can make stuff like that?

Mimura | (chuckling, shaking his head) No. My biggest seller is built on something my uncle wrote. All I did was tweak it a little.

Chisato | Is that what your uncle does for a living?

Mimura | No...

Mimura starts to say something but falls silent.

Chisato | (changing subjects) ...That guy—what a jerk, right?

Mimura | (smiling) You mean the one on the train? Yeah.

Chisato | He was taking up two seats for himself. And that old woman... Anyone could see she had weak legs.

Mimura | (laughs) Well, about now he's probably surrounded by the Youth Corps, getting told a thing or two. But if you ask me, I like the Youth Corps even less. Manners shouldn't be forced by the government or the community or anything. Having manners—and by that I mean being kind to others—is a good thing. But without understanding the

	beauty in virtue, it's all meaningless.
	Chisato's expression is a little unclear. The two enter the restaurant.
Waitress	Will there be two of you today? Will you be smoking?
Mimura	No. I quit. How about you?
Chisato	("I quit?") Of course not. (I'm in my school uniform. And a junior high school one at that.)
Waitress	This way, please.
	They take a booth next to the window.
Mimura	(handing Chisato the menu) Order whatever you like.
Chisato	I'm good with tea. Milk tea.
Mimura	Are you sure? You don't have to hold back.
Chisato	No, that's all right.
Mimura	Really? Okay...
	Mimura calls for the waitress.
Mimura	Umm...She'll have the milk tea, and I'll have the fruit takoyaki ice cream.
	It's actually on the menu.
Chisato	(What?!) (Her expression says: "What the heck is that?")
Mimura	I like the takoyaki sauce.
Chisato	Oh, um...okay.
	The waitress leaves their table, and the two look out the window where pedestrians and cars are passing by.
Chisato	I was coming from my lessons today.
Mimura	You mean like the tea ceremony?
Chisato	Yeah, tea and flower arranging, all of those kinds of things.
Mimura	Wow. But aren't there schools for that in Shiroiwa? Hmm...doesn't Kotohiki study tea or something?
Chisato	(with some surprise) (He does know a lot...about the girls.)
Mimura	What is it?
Chisato	Nothing. Anyway, the place I go is hosted by the Republic Nonaggressive Forces Wives Association. Have you heard of them?
Mimura	(shows her an ambiguous smile and clasps his hands together in the shape of a gun) Oh, you're one of those types? Look, I didn't mean—
Chisato	(hastily) It's not like that. I'm not into politics or anything like that. I just go because my parents make me.
	Mimura seems surprised.
Chisato	(nodding) I agree with the way you think, Mimura. Manners aren't

	something you force on others.
	Mimura's expression is ambiguous.
Chisato	But taking the lessons isn't all bad.
Mimura	(grinning) It looks good on your transcript?
Chisato	Well, that too, but... If I do really well, I can become a cultural ambassador, and I might be able to go outside the country.
Mimura	Wow, that is something.
Chisato (Cap)	In our country, the Republic of Greater East Asia, overseas travel is strictly regulated. The government doesn't think well of foreign "incorrect" information and culture.
Chisato	I want to see other countries. I want to see the many different worlds out there.
Mimura	(nodding) I see.... So that's why you study so hard at English.
Chisato	What? How did you...? (He knows?) My accent isn't even that good or anything.
Mimura	But you're always using that nice dictionary in class. And you listen so intently to the teacher. Anyone looking could see that.
Chisato	(blushing) (Does that mean he's been looking?) But you're good at English yourself. Aren't you interested in going to another country?
Mimura	The only English I know is broken—just what I need for my computer work...
	Mimura keeps it fairly vague.
Chisato	(frantically adding) Of course I don't think that other countries are better than this one, I just...
Mimura	(smiling) Is this a good country, when you're obligated to make excuses for it like that?
	Chisato lets out a little gasp.
Mimura	(chuckles and waves his hands) That's enough of the heavy talk... Now that I think about it, if I make the national team, I might be able to go out of the country too. If you and I go to the same place, then maybe we could share some tea like this. Like in a Parisian café. (grins)
	Chisato falls silent.
	The waitress brings the milk tea and the takoyaki ice cream.
Chisato	(looking at the takoyaki ice cream) ...
Waitress	Does this complete your order?
	But Mimura stops her.
Waitress	Yes?
Mimura	Um... That boy, over there. He's been alone this whole time.

Chisato looks and sees a boy, about seven or eight years old, sitting alone, two booths down and across the aisle. On his table is only a single glass of ice water.

Mimura — **Where's his mother? Is he all right?**

Waitress — **...A lot of children have been coming in by themselves lately. He's a regular. Very smart too. He's already finished his meal... Now, is there anything else?**

The waitress leaves.

Mimura — **I feel kind of bad for the kid.**

Mimura looks at the boy. The boy happens to glance up. Mimura makes a gun with his hand and pretends to shoot the boy. The boy grins, and Shinji grins back.

Mimura — **(facing Chisato, affecting a whisper) Watch out, he could be secret police, eavesdropping on our conversation.**

Chisato — **(dryly laughing) He could be.**

Act 2 The Battle

Satomi — **(as before, aiming her gun toward the school) No boys. We all decided that together.**

Chisato — **(slightly panicked) But come on, when Noriko was shot, he tried to help her. He told that Sakamochi guy that because Noriko was hurt, the experiment should be postponed.**

Satomi — **That could have been an act—just to get us to trust him.**

Kyoichi Motobuchi leaves the school and is shocked by the sight of Akamatsu's and Tendo's bodies.

Kyoichi — **Eeeaaaiiieeee!**

Kyoichi takes off running. He ducks into the thicket opposite from the girls, and the sound of rustling leaves fades into the distance.

Chisato is still having trouble accepting that Mimura has gone. She feels a hand on her shoulder and turns to see Yuka Nakagawa.

Yuka — **There's nothing you can do. Katsu—you know, Hatakami—he came out not that long ago. We're neighbors and were friends when we were little.**

Tears form in Yuka's eyes. Haruka also looks sad with her eyes down. Just then, someone approaches from the other thicket. Yukie and Satomi quickly aim their weapons.

Chisato's eyes widen. It's Shinji Mimura. He has a gun in his left hand, but he has both palms turned up and is showing no intent to use it.

Satomi — **Yukie—should we shoot?**

Yukie | **Wait.**

Mimura looks toward the girls. In the darkness of the undergrowth, he shouldn't be able to see Chisato, but his gaze nevertheless finds hers, and he grins. He turns around and flashes her the same three-finger gesture from the classroom and gives her a slight wave. Then he disappears back into the thicket.

Satomi | **(still aiming her gun in his direction) What...was that...?**

Chisato stares into the bushes where he vanished.

Mimura (Chisato's thought) | **Matsui, you're safer with Utsumi and the girls. Utsumi and the girls would never accept me. So I'm sorry, but this is goodbye.**

Chisato | **(crying) Ah... Ah...**

Yuka hugs Chisato's shoulder.

Act 2 End

Act 3 Pray

Back inside the restaurant.

Girl's Voice | **Oh! If it isn't Mimura!**

The voice belongs to one of a group of three girls. All are in winter tracksuits and appear to be in high school. She seems to have been sitting in one of the booths at the rear and spotted Mimura as she was leaving. She separates from her two friends and approaches. She's fairly pretty, with a kind of Latin feel. She's tall, and she even has large breasts!

Girl | **Long time no see. I was just thinking about calling you.**

The girl's eyes land on Chisato.

Mimura | **Oh, this is Chisato Matsui—from my class. We're on the health committee. Our teacher's injured, so we're paying him a visit, representing our class.**

Chisato | **(???)**

Chisato is confused but gives the girl a small bow.

Girl | **Oh, so that's it. I thought she might have been that younger sister you mentioned. 'Cause she's so little.**

Chisato | **... (Thanks for reminding me...)**

Girl | **I'm Kana Hotta. I play basketball at Takamatsu Vocational. Nice to meet you.**

Mimura | **Our teacher ruptured his Achilles tendon. He's a badminton coach, so the team's coming to meet us. We're waiting for them now.**

Chisato | **(Well, he's a smooth liar....)**

Hotta	Oh, okay. Well, sorry for butting in. (Looking to Chisato) It's too bad for me you're not his sister—I could have asked your advice about my future.
Chisato	...Your future?
Hotta	(blushing) Like, totally. He and I might get married someday. (turning back to Mimura) I'll be calling you for sure.
	The three girls leave the restaurant. We hear their voices: "This year, he was the MVP at the junior high prefectural tournament." "No way! So he's in junior high? Jailbait, huh?" "But he is cool!" Mimura is beaming.
Chisato	(eyes half lidded) Her chest...was so big.
Mimura	What? No, no, I know how that must have sounded...but I haven't done anything with her yet.
Chisato	("Yet," huh?) ("Her," huh?) But you're dating her, and you lied to her. All that about visiting our teacher, or whatever.
Mimura	Well...I'm not sure if we're exactly dating or not....Anyway, explaining this would've been a hassle, what with everything that's happened and all.
Chisato	(I wonder.)
Mimura	Anyway, don't be like that. She may not seem it, but she's been through a lot. Her parents divorced, for one thing. When we were in the seventh to twelfth grade prefecture-wide athletic camp, she came to me for advice.
Chisato	A high schooler came to someone in junior high for advice?
Mimura	Hey, it happens.
	Chisato shakes her head and sips her tea. Mimura takes a bite of his ice cream.
Mimura	So you should forgive her.
Chisato	Huh? For what?
Mimura	You know, how she said you were little.
Chisato	...
Mimura	She doesn't seem to like being as tall as she is. So when she said you were little, she didn't mean anything by it...I don't think.
	Chisato stirs her milk tea with her spoon a little.
Chisato	You don't seem to have any hang-ups, Mimura.
Mimura	Don't I?
Chisato	Well, you're good at sports and you get good grades. And you're popular with girls. And—
Mimura	(interrupting her) Every day—
Chisato	What?

Mimura — Every day, before I get out of my futon, I pray. Well, only for two or three minutes, but...

Chisato — You...pray?

Mimura — I ask that nothing bad happen that day. Then I finally get up.

Chisato — Umm...so...do you...well...believe in God?

Mimura — No. But, it's like... You know how Muslims are always praying way too much? I think I was just born the type of person who fits in with that. But even still, I hate religion, of course. I think anyone who claims they know what God is like is a fool. And yet I can't help but pray. Pretty sad, right?

Chisato — (hesitates, but asks anyway) Did something bad happen to you?

Mimura — (with a small chuckle) Well...I started spending a lot of time with my uncle, and he taught me everything, even basketball. And then I forgot the world was such a frightening place. But even still, I can't stop. In the morning, I pray.

Mimura is blushing a bit.

Mimura — Please don't tell anyone. No one knows but Yutaka–Seto, I mean. I haven't even told this to Nanahara.

Mimura eats a takoyaki ball. Chisato gazes down into her cup.

Mimura — I think one reason I do it is...just maybe...

Chisato looks up at him.

Mimura — ...when I was little, someone once said something to me. They said that some of my ancestors–distant, but ancestors–did something bad that made them rich, and that their wicked blood still ran inside me. I know it's not a big deal, but....

Chisato — (fairly incensed) It is a big deal! Who said that to you?

Mimura — (shrugging) You think so? Well...I guess Yutaka was furious when I told him, too.

Mimura eats a takoyaki ball. Chisato sips her tea.

Chisato — ...So you have a little sister?

Mimura — Yeah. Three years younger. Her name's Ikumi. She's a real smart-ass. What about you? Do you have any siblings?

Chisato — Yeah...an older brother...

Mimura — Oh yeah? I guess that makes us on the opposite end of things. What's your brother doing? Is he in our school? In high school?

Chisato — Well...I was born a bit after him.

Mimura — So college?

Chisato — (shakes her head)

Mimura — ...Still trying to get in?

Chisato — He was.

Mimura — **Was? What about now?**

Chisato sighs. She lifts up her tea spoon then sets it back down.

Chisato — **He died last year. He killed himself.**

Act 3 Interlude/The Battle

Kiriyama fires his Ingram wildly. Mimura is riddled by the bullets and slumps back against a box van.

Mimura (Cap) — **Yutaka...Uncle...Ikumi...**

Mimura (Cap) — **...Matsui.**

Mimura drops to his knees and falls forward. The farmers cooperative building is ablaze in the background.

* * *

Back in the restaurant.

Mimura — **Sorry. I didn't know.**

Chisato — **No. There was no reason for you to know. You weren't in my class last year. And it's a little different than if my parents had died. Only a few of my close friends came to the funeral. Of those in our class, I think just the class leader–Yukie–and Izumi attended.**

Mimura pushes his half-eaten ice cream to the side and calls the waitress over.

Mimura — **Excuse me. Could I get a coffee please?**

The coffee arrives quickly. Mimura adds milk but no sugar, stirs it, then takes a drink.

Chisato — **After my brother failed the college entrance exam, he got involved in some irregular things.**

Mimura drinks his coffee and lets her talk.

Chisato — **Do you know about anti-government groups?**

Mimura — **(with an ambiguous expression) Sure, I guess...**

Chisato — **(shakes her head) Now, I don't know what really happened. But the police came and took him in for questioning over it. Even after he returned, I never talked to him about the whole thing–and of course I never brought it up with my father or my mother. I think I was too scared to do it...I'm still scared now.**

Mimura — **But...since he was released, he mustn't have been involved. If he had been, even as a minor, he wouldn't have been let out for at least six months.**

Chisato — **(lifts her head and looks at Mimura) You sure know a lot. The detective told me the same thing.**

Mimura — I guess.

Chisato — After my brother came back...I don't know if I'd say he was a recluse, exactly, but...he kind of became that way. I certainly don't think he gave up on passing the exams. He was still buying prep books.

Mimura — Uh-huh.

Chisato — But...in the end, he went off on his own—without telling any of us. He only left a simple note.

Mimura — Oh?

Chisato — Yeah.

Chisato sits up straight and lets out a breath.

Chisato — I think that's why my parents made me start taking lessons from the Nonaggressive Forces Wives Association. They never really told me why and I never asked, but that's the only explanation, isn't it? I think it was a way for them to announce: "This girl's behavior is pure and proper. She's being schooled in the ideals of this great nation. She has absolutely no connection with any anti-government movement whatsoever."

Mimura — Uh-huh.

Chisato — I don't mind tea and flowers themselves. I rather like them, actually. I could maybe do without the reciting of the Leader's Analects, but we have to do that at school too anyway. But then today...

Mimura slowly sips his coffee as he watches Chisato's expression.

Chisato — ...someone said something to me. They said they heard that my brother was interrogated by the police. After all, Shiroiwa's not far from here. Word must have gotten out.

Mimura — That's cold. What's the point in someone bringing that up?

Chisato — (smiling sadly) Thanks. Sorry. All I'm doing is complaining.

Mimura — Complain away. If you can make do with me, I'll be your listener for a million hours.

Chisato — A million hours?

Mimura — Yeah. I'll listen forever.

Chisato smirks.

Mimura — What?

Chisato — You can't do that. Don't you have to go on a date with Hotta?

Mimura — Eh? Ah, well...Yeah, but...

Now Chisato straight out laughs.

Then the boy sitting two booths down glances out the window and stands. His mother must have come. The boy nods to someone outside the window and walks to the register. As he passes by Mimura and Chisato, he stops for a moment.

Boy — You're not going to visit your teacher. You're on a date, right?

Mimura — (laughing) Bingo. You come here a lot? If we see each other again and you're not busy, you wanna play basketball with me? I'm pretty good.

The boy grins. He forms a gun with his hand, points it at Mimura, and then leaves the restaurant.

Mimura — He was secret police after all. He was listening.

Chisato — (grinning) Yeah. But, Mimura...you lied again.

Mimura — That was no lie. At least not today.

Chisato — Huh?

Mimura — If it looks like a date to other people, then that's what it is. Oh...

Chisato — What?

Mimura — The train. We'll have to wait for the next one.

Chisato — (checking her watch) Yeah... That's okay.

Mimura — Are you starting to feel like you're under my spell?

Chisato — Don't worry. I've got the "absolute national defense sphere" of the A cup.

Mimura — (grinning) Well, in that case, you wanna take a walk with me until it's time? There's a river nearby.

Act 3 End

Act 4 Burn

The two leave the restaurant and are walking down a sidewalk alongside the river when Mimura speaks.

Mimura — My uncle also died last year.

Chisato looks surprised.

Mimura — They say it was an accident, but it seems a little fishy to me.

Chisato listens without speaking.

Mimura — My uncle was involved with anti-government activities.

The two arrive at a bridge. Not far from the sea, the river is muddy here.

Mimura — This river's filthy.

They cross the bridge then walk along the base of the concrete embankment at the water's edge.

Mimura — Anyway, there was this woman in Marugame who had been close to my uncle. She's been dead a long time now, but one of her relatives was putting her belongings in order recently when he found some of my uncle's letters. He called me up and asked if I could come and get them. I was actually closer to my uncle than my father was, and my uncle never married. So I came to retrieve his letters. Hmm...

Mimura seems to be looking for something along the river.

Chisato

What is it?

Mimura

Oh, well... Ah... There it is. It's over there. I noticed it before.

Mimura starts to walk briskly. He passes through a gap in the guard rail and out onto a part of the concrete that for some reason juts a little way out into the river. On the edge of the concrete platform is a kerosene canister with its lid cut off and removed. Blackened with soot and holding ashes within, the canister seems to have been previously used to burn trash. There are also two empty cans of juice inside, but these look completely unscathed.

Mimura

Let's use this little guy.

Mimura removes the juice cans.

Chisato

...Are you burning something? Won't we get in trouble doing that in the middle of the city?

Mimura

The whole of Takamatsu is country. It'll be fine.

Mimura pulls a single large envelope from his bag and dumps its entire contents into the canister, all of them letters.

Chisato

Those are...

Mimura

They're letters that my uncle wrote to her.

Chisato

You're going to burn them? Why? Do they all have something dangerous written in them?

Mimura

No, it's not like that. Even if my uncle had really been involved in anything actually dangerous, our mail's always getting opened, so anything of that nature would have been used as evidence against him. They're just love letters.

Chisato

But even love letters are important, aren't they?

Mimura

The letters were important to them. But they're both gone now. You know how sometimes people find the love letters of some old composer or something? Even though they were meant to be private? It's humiliating.

Chisato

Maybe you're right, but still...

Mimura

Well, whether it's humiliating or not is beside the point. What I'm trying to say is that what they felt for each other belongs only to them.

Mimura takes out his lighter, picks up one of the letters, sets it alight and tosses it in.

Mimura

I especially don't want the government officials or cops getting their filth all over these.

Chisato

That's why you said we needed to get off the train.

Mimura	That's right.
	The flames grow.
Chisato	Anyway, there sure are a lot. They must have really loved each other.
Mimura	(with a small chuckle) No. Apparently, she was seeing someone. My uncle's was a one-sided love.
Chisato	What? But...
Mimura	This is only partly my guess, but...the guy she was with was deep into anti-government activities.
Chisato	Really?
Mimura	Really. And he was executed for it. Since she was dating him, they obviously investigated her. After that, she had a mental breakdown... Though I'm sure the shock of her loved one's death was a part of it.
Chisato	...
Mimura	I only looked at the dates on the stamps' cancellations. Not even counting the really old ones, there were 46 sent over the course of a single year—one a week for 46 weeks.
Chisato	...
Mimura	She committed suicide. The woman my uncle loved killed herself before the 46th letter arrived. That was the only one unopened.
	Chisato looks up at Mimura's face. Mimura watches the flames.
Mimura	Before she died, she sent her earrings to my uncle, as a memento, I guess. They came with a note, on which she'd only written, "Thank you."
	Mimura points at his left ear.
Mimura	Actually, this is one of them. I guess it's kind of a subleased memento, huh? The other one's in my uncle's grave.
	Mimura looks to Chisato. She is crying.
Chisato	My brother wrote the same thing in his note. He addressed it to my father, my mother and me. It said, "Thank you."
Mimura	...Oh.
Chisato	But I wasn't able to do anything for my brother. Not like what your uncle did for her. After my brother was detained, I just tiptoed around him.
Mimura	...
Chisato	It was because of him that I became interested in other countries. He had lots of foreign books, and he showed me that the world is a big place. But I....
Mimura	That's not true. I'm sure your brother was glad just to have you there. I'm a big brother myself, so I understand.

Chisato | (crying more) ...I don't know.

Mimura | It's true.

Chisato wipes her eyes.

Chisato | ...I don't care what anyone says to me... I just wish he was still alive...

Mimura | ...That's what my uncle said too.

Inside the kerosene canister, the letters are burning. One line, "Do you remember?" is visible for a moment, but is quickly swallowed by the fire.

Chisato | Mimura...why are you telling me all this, when it means so much to you?

Mimura | You told me about your brother, right? It's only fair.

Chisato | But before that, why did you tell me about your prayers?

Mimura | ...Hmm...well, there was something about you today. You looked like a balloon about to fly away. Maybe I just thought I could say something to catch you. I felt that way when I saw you on the platform at Ritsurin Station.

Chisato cries even more. Mimura takes the outside of one of her arms.

Mimura | I'm just holding you up, that's all. It's okay, right? I'm not going to make a pass at you. I keep my promises.

Chisato | ...Okay.

Mimura | Hey, if I were your big brother. I wouldn't want you to fly away.

Chisato | Okay.

Mimura | There's something else my uncle said to me once. Don't let yourself be blown about. When you fly, leap for yourself. Do it on your own terms, and when the moment is right.

Chisato | Yeah...

Mimura | Go to another country, someday, and see it with your own eyes. If you do that, I'm sure your brother will be happy.

Chisato | Yeah...Yeah...

The flames have died down now.

Chisato | (wiping her tears) But with you holding my arm like this, it really is like you've arrested me.

Shinji | Come in, headquarters. The suspect is in custody. The suspect is in custody. She was making a fire beside the river.

Chisato | Ha ha ha ha.

Act 4 The Battle

Six a.m. on the 23rd.

Sakamoto (P.A.) **Your new dead friends are: Iijima, Oda, Seto and...Mimura.**

* * *

Atop the lighthouse, Yukie Utsumi and Haruka Tanizawa show their faces from the doorway. Chisato is on watch. The two approach Chisato. She's crying.

Act 4 End

Act 5 Fly

Mimura and Chisato walk toward the station.

Mimura **Hey, Matsui. Here, take this.**

He hands her a scrap of paper with something written on it.

Mimura **It's my email address. If you're ever in serious need of a hand, you can reach me there.**

Chisato **...Okay.**

Shinji **But if it looks like trouble, be sure to ditch that note. If you could memorize it, that would be the best.**

Chisato stares at the note for a moment, then returns it to Mimura.

Mimura **You memorized that already? Incredible.**

Chisato **If nothing else, I have a good memory.**

Mimura **All right.**

Mimura takes the scrap of paper, crumples it, and stuffs it back into his pocket.

Mimura **We're friends now.**

Chisato **(bashfully) Oh...Yeah.**

Mimura **But with what happened with your brother and what happened with my uncle, I think we're better off not talking or anything at school.**

Chisato **Yeah... You're right.**

Mimura **So, today, we'll be taking the same train and bus back home, but that's only a coincidence. Once we're back in Shiroiwa, we need to act like nothing happened. Got it?**

Chisato **Yeah.**

They arrive at the station. A little time is left before the next train comes. Shinji buys their tickets, and they sit on an open bench.

Mimura	I don't feel like you're going to fly away...not anymore.
Chisato	Yeah.
Mimura	When you fly...
Chisato	I'll leap for myself, and when the moment is right.
Mimura	All right. That's how it is.

* * *

Chisato (Cap) And that's how it was. After that, in school, Mimura and I didn't talk or anything.

Chisato (Cap) But sometimes, he would give me a sign that only I would understand.

The two pass in the school hallway. Chisato is talking with her girlfriends, and Mimura is talking to Shuya Nanahara and his friends. But where Chisato can see it, Mimura lifts his hand a little and stands up his thumb, pointer and middle fingers.

Chisato has come to watch Mimura's basketball game. She's wearing a hat, a muffler and glasses as a sort of disguise. A group of girls—Mimura's would-be groupies—are in the stands. But after he scores another basket and responds to his fans' cries, his back is turned to Chisato when he raises his right hand in that gesture.

Chisato (He noticed me!) (He saw through my disguise!)

Chisato (Cap) I continued my lessons with the Wives Association, and that's how I happened to see something nice.

Chisato is walking near that restaurant. She sees, inside a park, Mimura playing basketball with that little boy. He even seems to have brought a child-sized ball.

Chisato (Cap) Mimura kept his promise. (Of course, he might have been in the area after coming to see that girl Hotta.)

Chisato smiles and resumes walking.

Act 5 The Battle

Satomi Who did it? Which one of you tried to kill us?

Yukie Calm down. This is all a misunderstanding.

Satomi A misunderstanding?

The group of girls have three guns between them: the Uzi submachine gun held by Satomi, the Browning semi-automatic pistol tucked into the back of Yukie's skirt (Yukie doesn't have her hand on it yet), and the CZ 75 semi-automatic pistol lying atop the sideboard. Chisato sees Haruka glance at the CZ.

Chisato This is bad. Yukie is still being rational, but if Haruka takes that gun and points it at Satomi, then...

Chisato That's it–if I throw it out the window, Satomi should understand.

* * *

Chisato remembers Mimura telling her:

Mimura — **Leap for yourself. On your own terms, and when the moment is right.**

* * *

Chisato — **I have to leap now.**

Chisato runs to the CZ.

Chisato — **I have to take it and throw it far away.**

But Satomi's machine gun spits fire, and Chisato is slammed against the sideboard.

Chisato — **What...?**

Chisato's vision swims.

Chisato — **Oh...I see...Satomi thought I was going to take the gun and shoot her. How...stupid am I...?**

Yukie — **Satomi! What are you doing?!**

Haruka — **Yukie! Stop her. Stop Satomi!**

And more gunfire. But Chisato hears neither their voices or the gunfire anymore.

Chisato — **Mimura...I failed...Even though I finally leaped for myself...I'm such a fool...**

Act 5 Postlude

Mimura and Chisato are still waiting for the train at Matsushima Sanchome Station when a young man in a school uniform (the one talking to the elderly man in Act 2) approaches. He has plastic-frame glasses, dweebish unkempt hair and a camera.

Young Man — **Um...excuse me.**

Mimura — **Yes?**

Young Man — **My name's Yoshino, and I'm studying photography at the Creative Arts High School. I'm learning portraits right now and you two, uh... look like a nice couple. I was wondering if you'd mind letting me take your picture.**

Mimura and Chisato exchange a glance. Then Mimura looks back at Yoshino.

Mimura — **Will you end up doing an exhibition or something? If the picture's only for practice and you won't show it outside school—even if it turns out good—then I don't mind.**

Yoshino — **Understood. I promise I won't publish it outside school.**

Chisato (under her breath, to Mimura) Are you sure it's okay?

Shinji It'll be fine. On the off chance it gets out, we just met here today by chance anyway. We just happened to meet and happened to model for a student. It's all a coincidence.

The two stand next to each other on the station platform.

Yoshino Oh, and actually, I have one more favor to ask.

Mimura (spreading open his arms) What's that?

Yoshino I'm doing a theme where I'm having all my subjects jump. Now, you don't have to overdo it or anything—just be jumping when I press the shutter. Can you do that?

Mimura and Chisato exchange another look.

Chisato I'm fine with that.

Mimura points at Yoshino's camera.

Mimura That's a 28mm lens, right? So you're gonna have to back up to take it right.

Yoshino Huh? But...

Shinji I play some sports, and I've had a little experience behind a camera. I'll definitely be out of frame.

Yoshino Oh, okay. I see.

Yoshino steps back.

Yoshino All right, well, um...what do you want to do for a signal?

Shinji I'll count it down. One, two, three, daah.

Chisato (Daah?)

Shinji (looking over his shoulder at Chisato) I'm really gonna jump, Matsui. Okay?

Chisato Okay.

Shinji So jump high.

Chisato Okay.

Shinji looks ahead and holds up his right hand.

Mimura One, two, three...

On one, Mimura sticks up his pointer finger; on two, his middle finger; and on three, his thumb. (This is the sign he will be giving to Chisato later.)

Yoshino Whoa! (with an astonished expression)

We see the photo. Mimura is indeed jumping high, as if making a jump shot toward the basket. Chisato is looking up at him, smiling, as she too jumps.

End

Afterword

Wow, having an assistant credit after my name makes me feel cool, like mine is the name of a band. And, well, I did have an ulterior motive (yes, really) of temporarily obscuring the answer to that most peculiar question: "Is Koushun Takami still alive?" But now that I've written this afterword, the secret's out! The secret's out! (I repeat.)

Most readers of this book probably don't know that I mentioned the story of Episode 1 in the afterword of the 2009 edition of the North American translation of the *Battle Royale* novel. I wrote that I had an idea for a scene with two of the girls talking atop the lighthouse, but that I wouldn't go back and add to my novel's story. Well, didn't I just do that! Didn't I just do that! (I repeat.)

Episode 2 was created almost entirely from scratch for this book, though I quickly realized that Chisato Matsui's connection with Shinji Mimura was perhaps all I had left to explore. Any readers who thought I was inspired by Kiyoshiro Imawano's "JUMP" probably noticed it straightaway, but regardless, thanks to the stern urgings of X-san in Editorial, I was able to get the story into shape. X-san, thank you. More thanks to N-san, also in charge of editing this manga; M-san, who was in charge of the earlier *Battle Royale* manga (Masayuki Taguchi's version); K-san; and everyone else at Akita Publishing. And of course, my heartfelt thanks also go to Ohnishi-san and Oguma-san. Thank you for sticking with me through the end despite my selfishness. And thank you to my sworn friend, N-Cake, whose imagery expanded the boundaries of my imagination. At first I thought of this project as a gift to celebrate M-san's advancement to lead editor, but by the end it turned out that the person to whom it was the greatest gift—and yes, maybe I should have known—was me. It was me. (I repeat.)

As I write this, twelve—nearly thirteen—years have passed since the publication of *Battle Royale* the novel. Over such a long period of time, many things have happened, and several people important to me have passed (Robert B. Parker and Saeko Himuro among them). Of course, the vast number of people who have died having no connection to me, and who range from the famous to the unknown, are each important to other people out there somewhere. There's been 9/11 and 3/11, and while more must inform our views of an event than solely the number of fatalities, what perhaps impacts us most is when deaths we typically ignore are forced upon us in a form we can easily understand. In truth, each and every death carries deep and overwhelming meaning, regardless of whether or not it becomes a news headline. But despite all this—or rather, because of it:

If you and I are still alive, and we meet again one day, that's far more important, don't you think? I can't say I live a proper, respectable life, but I'm still living—are you? Well, if more time passes and we both are still alive, let's meet again.

I'm still living. Are you still living? (I repeat.)

Autumn 2011
Koushun Takami

KOUSHUN TAKAMI was born in 1969 in Amagasaki near Osaka and grew up in Kagawa Prefecture of Shikoku, where he currently resides. After graduating from Osaka University with a degree in literature, he dropped out of Nihon University's liberal arts correspondence-course program. From 1991 to 1996 he worked for the prefectural news company Shikoku Shinbun, reporting on various fields, including politics, police reports, and economics. Although he has an English teaching certificate, he has yet to visit the United States.

Battle Royale, completed after Takami left the news company, was rejected in the final round of a literary competition sponsored by a major publisher due to the critical controversy it provoked among jury members. With its publication in Japan in 1999, though, *Battle Royale* received widespread support, particularly from young readers, and became a best seller. In 2000, *Battle Royale* was serialized as a comic and made into a feature film.

Mr. Takami is currently working on his second novel.

MIOKO OHNISHI debuted with the one-shot "Needful Needles" in Akita Shoten's *Monthly Shonen Champion* and is drawing the manga adaptation of Baku Yumemakura's *Shamon Kukai Tou no Kuni ni te Oni to Utagesu*, Volume 1 of which is available from Kadokawa Digital Comics.

YOUHEI OGUMA debuted with the one-shot "Sekai ha Kyo mo Kantansou ni Mawaru" in Akita Shoten's *Young Champion*. He has had several one-shots featured in Young Champion and *Monthly Young Champion Retsu*.

BATTLE ROYALE ANGELS' BORDER

VIZ Signature Edition

Story by Koushun Takami (with N-Cake)
Art by Mioko Ohnishi & Youhei Oguma

English Translation & Adaptation // Nathan Collins
Touch-up Art & Lettering // Annaliese Christman
Design // Fawn Lau
Editor // Pancha Diaz

First published in Japan in 2012 by Akita Publishing Co., Ltd., Tokyo
English translation rights arranged with Akita Publishing Co., Ltd.

Printed in the U.S.A.

Published by VIZ Media, LLC
P.O. Box 77010
San Francisco, CA 94107

10 9 8 7 6 5 4 3 2 1
First printing, June 2014

viz
media
www.viz.com

RATED
T+
FOR OLDER TEEN
PARENTAL ADVISORY
BATTLE ROYALE: ANGELS' BORDER is rated T+ for Older Teen and is recommended for ages 16 and up. This volume contains violence.
ratings.viz.com

VIZ SIGNATURE

This is the LAST PAGE

BATTLE ROYALE ANGELS' BORDER HAS BEEN PRINTED IN THE ORIGINAL JAPANESE FORMAT IN ORDER TO PRESERVE THE ORIENTATION OF THE ORIGINAL WORK.